The Book Of Obsidian

Delizhia Jenkins

OTHER BOOKS BY DELIZHIA JENKINS:

Frostbite, Slay

THE BOOK OF OBSIDIAN
I:I

There are gifts of Heaven such as the dawn; the night sky and life in and of itself. But there are curses: Curses that stain the night and blot out even the light of the stars. Her curse is many – as many as the names she holds.

SACRED SCRIPTURES TAKEN FROM THE PAGES OF THE BOOK OF OBSIDIAN

Book of Obsidian 1:2: *She breathes fire; but she was born of a celestial body – this is the result of life's spark. Death fears her, while life cowers at the mere mention of her name.*

Book of Obsidian 1:3: *She wears several rings and rules over empires of death. She swings her Scythe in the name of Harvest while bearing the mark of the Reaper.*

Book of Obsidian 1:4: *A Reaper is a collector of lost things; but Kalima is the Harvester of Sins.*

Book of Obsidian 1:5: *The armies of Heaven and Hell will lay siege to her throne of Darkness only to fall; just as the armies of the earth.*

Book of Obsidian 1:6: *She who is the Destroyer of worlds, with the spin of her Scythe is the answer to the call of both Death and Life.*

Book of Obsidian 1:7: *Her rage is like that of a cloud of locusts devouring a field. It is unmerciful, relentless and unforgiving. The dark* *trembles at her feet, bowing to her whim. She is like that of a nightmare with no end.*

Book of Obsidian 1:8*: Destroyer of life but born of pure Light. She is the broken star that swallows the night. Angels watch for her; for when she comes it is because Fate had been tested. Her true name is Genesis.*

Book of Obsidian 2:1*: He that reads this warning shall be given hope that the Trinity does not come to pass. Her strength, her power taken from by the separation of the Book and the Scythe...*

Book of Obsidian 2:2*: The Scythe is the Harvester; and the Book is the Bringer. Heed this warning: Those who possess the Book will awaken her power and should she possess the Scythe, she will awaken Death.*

Book of Obsidian 2:3*: Sin is the beacon for Obsidian. She is the result from the birth of a dark force; a force so dark and abysmal demons flee from it. No angel dare to venture to her realm.*

Book of Obsidian 2:4*: She will lead an army of Reapers. Each of the Black Winged Scythe Bearers at her Mercy. And hell will be unleashed onto the earth.*

Book of Obsidian 2:5*: Her Awakening will mark the rise of the Old gods.*

Book of Obsidian 2:6*: And then she will turn to the Heavens to bring justice to the Heavens and stars. She will Reap the Harvest of the cosmos and even the angels will know not of what more will come.*

Book of Obsidian 2:7: *Her instrument of Death will turn valleys into dust; rivers into blood as the earth itself will melt away from her touch. Rivers will beg for mercy as the oceans utter a silent plea of sorrow.*

Book of Obsidian: 2:8: *She will Awaken to the cry of man; she will carry righteous fury in her right hand. She is the bringer of balance.*

Book of Obsidian 2:9: *Even the angels know not the power she will bring. If one were to utter the words of her Scythe, the cosmos will bow at his feet.*

Book of Obsidian 2:10: *The power of her Scythe will unleash her army of Reapers igniting a war between them and the Archangels. The Reapers shall cast the Archangels into the Pond of Darkness, stripping them of their light and Heaven will exist no more.*

Book of Obsidian 2:11: *She came before the Nine and was sought to bring balance unto the Old Gods. She was to become the restorer of Justice and the Guardian Protector of the Nine Gateways*

Book of Obsidian 2:12: *She was created before the angels; presented as a gift of vengeance.*

Book of Obsidian 2:13: *The first of the Nine Gateways is Time. Her Scythe is the Key to Gateway One; Once her Scythe begins its spin, all will reset. Time will unlock and reverse creating a portal of destruction.*

Book of Obsidian 2:14: *She will rise like the fire of the Phoenix when the Nine awakens. For the Awakening of the Nine will summon her to call forth the power of her Scythe.*

Book of Obsidian 2:15: *It is the power of her Scythe the Nine seek; and it is havoc on earth that the Nine will wreak. A war between the gods and the Spirits of man will release the souls of the Damned.*

Book of Obsidian 2:16: *The bowels of Hell will open and split apart, and the earth will tremble and shake. Her temple and her throne will be built from the blaze.*

Book of Obsidian 2:17: *When the Nine awakens, her Scythe will spin, stirring up the winds from all four corners of the earth. The seas will howl for her mercy and the stars will collapse from the sky. Darkness will part from the night and even the demons in hell will scream in fright.*

Book of Obsidian 2:18: *Those whose eyes fall upon the pages of this book will unleash her power. And should she be set free before the alignment of Karma, War, Nightmares and Death, may the being responsible breath his last breath.*

Book of Obsidian 3:1: *The Flames of the sun will add fire to the funeral pyre where the Nine will face their judgement.*

Book of Obsidian 3:2: *And from the darkened path of the sky, in the hallowed spaces behind the sun, the Serpent will awaken. His staff will rise to the call of Kalima's Scythe; and upon the end of Kalima's destructive rage, the balance of life and death will be assuaged.*

Book of Obsidian 3:3: *They will come, the Nine and wage war with the Heavens. They will bring ruin to each realm across the galaxies. They* will awaken old gods who have been locked away and it is here those eyes which stumble across this book begins the fulfillment of the prophecy.

Book of Obsidian 3:4: *The keeper of the Serpent hand will rattle the stars in response to her command. Ophiuchus, the Dark One will restore the light, completing a prophesy of an endless night.*

Book of Obsidian 3:5: *A war of the Heavens shall shake the stars from the sky; and the earth will rumble as more sleeping gods rise. Beware Calypso, High Priestess of Prophecy. She will awaken with a vengeance and shall part the stars like the red sea. She will bring destruction to Heaven above and Hell below, she is but a curse to the cosmos.*

Book of Obsidian 3:6: *Orion, the Keeper of the Gates will side with Kalima to unleash the power of the Serpent to form a Trinity. The power of Obsidian has spoken. Take heed.*

Book of Obsidian: 3:7: *Orion, Keeper of the Gates will side with Kalima to unleash the power of the Serpent. Beware the worshippers of the Fallen! Take heed ye old betrayers of Truth. Thy souls be damned, you must repent.*

Book of Obsidian 3:8: *Beware the treachery of a Fallen. His tongue is as cunning as the serpent who glides on his belly devouring truths and spitting out lies. His ruin will befall the Nine.*

Book of Obsidian 3:9: *For those who dare to open the pages of this book shall it be undone. The power of the Scythe will spin against the hands of time; the seeker of Kalima's power will then rise. But if it is Kalima who is awakened shall the end begin. Ophiuchus, Orion and Kalima, the Cleansers of sin. For if it is Kalima who awakens, it is because the Nine have called and Titus will be the first of the Nine to Fall. Her power is in* *the Black Sun, known as Obsidian. Pas op vir die swart son (Beware the Black Sun)*

Book of Obsidian 4:1: ካሊማ ፤ ጥቁር የፀሐይ ጥቁር አምላክ ሁሉም ዘጠኝ ፕላኔቶች በአንድ ሌሊት ሲቀራረቡ የመጽሐፉ መወረድ ጥርጥር የለበትም ፡ ፡ ከዓለማት ጌታ ነው ፡ ፡ እስክትነቃ ድረስ እነዚህን ገጾች ይጠብቁ ፡፡ ይህ መጽሐፍ በተሳሳተ እጅ ቢወድቅ ኃይሏ ይጠፋል፡፡

Translation: Kalima, dark goddess of the black sun when all nine planets align in a single night. The keeper of this book shall inherit her Scythe. Protect these pages, until she awakens. Should this book fall into the wrong hands, her power will be taken.

Your purpose is always greater than your pain.
Remember that.

PROLOGUE

Kalima

"Michael, move immediately!" Archangel Gabriel snarled as he gathered his gigantic white wings about him and descended from the heavens, closing in behind me like a shooting star.

"Confiscate her! She cannot escape!" A swarm of Archangels, Heaven's Elite combat fighting force took form above me. Their eyes fueled with the anger of the sun; resolve spurred them to stop the hands of what I believed to be destiny.

I leaped over a chasm and fired another blast of my black rage at the two archangels who sought to obstruct my way. I'd had enough. For what reason was I created to merely be secreted away, to become nothing more than a dead prophesy just because mankind has demonstrated that there may be another path? *This* was my fate.

I smashed my feet into the ground and the earth

rumbled before it broke apart as I tore my way across the gorge. *Humans were nothing more than wastes of flesh and bone*, I fumed to myself. *They killed for pleasure just as much as they fucked for pleasure; the damned tended to rule the weak while the meek and mild perished from suffering.*

Summoning my Scythe into my grip, I spun it, fueling it with my dark rage. For centuries I had slept, trapped in my own dreamworld of paradise, under the spell of the Creator who knew that the day of my awakening would come. Over time, the desperate cries from the humans would filter their way into my dreamscape. There were days that I would lay on the lush green grass of the fields and gaze at the sun. There were also nights when I would sit naked and alone under the light of the moon, wondering if the other gods and lords of the darker realms knew that I existed. I yearned for contact, for touch, for a word... But even during those moments when I felt most alone, I was still at peace.

And then the piercing scream of a human child cut through the silence of the sun.

I began to observe the race of humans by stepping out into the creek where I could see from behind the Veil and connect with those beings who resided beyond the dreamscape. Curious creatures they were...I spent many a night studying them, often focusing on a single group and observing them well beyond their life spans. I grew to empathize with their struggles and often petitioned the heavens on their behalf. From my dreamscape world, I often would send guides and messengers in the form of my favorite winged creature – the crow- to assist when needed. In time humans soon recognized my presence and some had learned from their masters how to harness their own power and communicate with those of us hidden in the worlds between.

I've been called many names throughout the ages, but on this eve, only the angels will remember me as *the* Great Cleanser. I can taste the sin that hangs in the air. No more. No more murder. No more tears. And no more worshipping of gods who despised men. The latter is what all these fools fail to understand. They overlooked the fact that there was something greater than all of them that was coming. HE was coming. THEY would follow.

"You cannot stop me Michael nor you Gabriel!" I shouted as the wind began to pick up in speed.

"Kalima..." The deep velvety voice of a soul that even in my blackened rage, could never ever hurt. "Please don't do this..."

I could feel him behind me, my Asir. My dear sweet Asir. The only male who understood my depths and watered my spirit with his love. He was neither human nor god, but somehow existed in both the flesh and spirit.

"Asir... once my Scythe begins to spin, this cycle of earth, this realm, and all that must come to an end," I remind him softly. "You must go. Go to The Veil and stay there until my return. I do not want you harmed here."

"You cannot harm me," he told me, placing his warm hand on my shoulder. "But the angels and the lords... the masters have spoken. You are not to execute the prophecy before its time. It is not your destiny to do so Kalima."

"I possess a fate that you could never understand...They knew what I was when I was created. They knew me before I knew of my power, and they cast me into a deep slumber only for me to awaken to my fury when the time came. How can I not be fulfilling a prophecy that they knew would happen?"

I could sense Michael and his band of loyalists closing in on me from above and with a twist of my wrist I sent another shockwave of power that blew them out of the sky.

"I'm so sorry my love," I heard Asir whisper to me. "But I cannot let you do this..." The sharpness of a cursed obsidian dagger pierced straight through the muscles and tendons of my back and into my heart. The pain of both his actions and the actual betrayal itself could not be matched. I felt my power drain from my hands just as my blood dripped from my wound. My Scythe slowly came to a stop only to collapse on the ground in front of me. Clutching my chest, I dropped to my knees and studied my blood soaked hands. Asir's mournful wails wrapped around me. His pain became mine and mine his. He wanted to protect the world from me, from my power... but his gentle heart could never fathom that the world didn't need protection, it needed my help.

"I love you Kalima. I will love you in this life and the next and so forth... but right now, you cannot exist here..."

Death is a rebirth; and it is in death where I am reborn. Asir sent me back to the dreamscape, where my spirit could be one with the sun and moon. But he never returned to me. He left me alone, seemingly content with us to be separated by the Veil... that is, until my spirit was once again called forth to be born in the flesh. Yet, my spirit would remain sleeping, resting peacefully in the physical form of a human in a world where gods no longer walked among men but were men. And these men would soon learn what it would mean to bow before a greater god.

Dinayra

"Are you alright Dinayra?"

Another night, another migraine, at least that is what I tell myself even though the strength of this headache is beyond anything I have experienced. Bile makes its way up my throat, and I rush to the bathroom just in time to upchuck the last of what I ate for lunch. Tears fill my eyes as I press the handle of the toilet and flush. "Fuck…"

"Baby, you sure we shouldn't go back to the hospital?" Cairo asks me from the doorway.

"No. I just need to take what he has already given me and lay down for a while." The Tylenol codeines were no longer effective and whatever leftover opioids I was prescribed wouldn't get me through the night. I just spent the last 48 hours in an emergency room with every kind of test available being conducted on me.

And nothing. The doctors found nothing.

These unexplainable but reoccurring migraines have haunted

7

me for most of my life. Poor Cairo, he has been suffering with me since the day he and I first met. The moment our eyes connected on the busy streets of Downtown Los Angeles, I collapsed with a seizure. Strangely enough, he has been by my side since. Throughout the years the episodes slowly increased in strength and frequency, even with the prescribed medication.

"The tea that I made you last time help right?" he asked from the doorway as another round of nausea held me face first over the toilet.

"It did," I breathed. Sucking in another hard breath I fought to regain my composure.

"Good. I always keep the special herb concoctions with me..."

Bile builds back up in my throat and like a volcano, I erupt. It feels never ending, and my question is how? I hardly ate anything today. Cairo disappears and after another round of flushes, I can barely stand up. My head is spinning and pushing myself away from the toilet seems impossible. Slinking to the floor, I manage to lean against the wall and focus my breath to rebuild my strength.

"Babe, your tea is almost ready!" Cairo calls from down the hall.

"Ok," I croak. My throat burns with my reply and I wonder just how much of esophagus do I have left? Every fiber of my body just wants to crawl into my bed and remain there until the world ends. Thankfully my job has been understanding of my current situation. My boss just figured the episodes were related to stress and offered me quite a bit of time off for medical leave. I hope she is right with her assumption.

With what remained of my strength, I begin crawling out of the bathroom – which even with me on all fours felt like a road trip to China – on foot. Each muscle cried out to rest while I moved like an aging snail across the linoleum floor. However, after what felt like forever and a day, I managed to make it to my bedroom, where

I gave up the fight less than a foot away from my bed. The carpet felt welcoming anyway and perhaps at some point today, I might make it between the sheets.

"Your tea is…" I can feel Cairo's presence in the doorway. "Dinayra!" He rushes forward, careful not to spill the cup of tea when he sat it down on my dresser. His warm strong hands gently lift me off the floor and place me on the bed. He tucks me under my favorite navy- blue comforter I bought from a flea market.

"Are you sure you don't want to go back to the hospital? Nothing about this seems normal."

"Just let me rest babe," I groan closing my eyes.

He leans down and places a gentle kiss on my forehead. "You're burning up…"

"Comes with the territory…"

"D, I don't like this. But I will let you rest for a while. I will be back in an hour to check on you."

I can sese his reluctance to leave, but he's been down this road with me on more than one occasion. The pain is far too draining to continue the fight to remain conscious. Even my bones feel weak. Exhaustion becomes my guide and directs me towards the path of deep slumber. Eventually, I find myself slipping away, the sound of my own deep breaths a calming lullaby.

And then the familiar voice that has haunted me since childhood returned but instead of sweeping away the nightmares that plagued me, she stood waiting for me at the edge of a cliff, overlooking the spaces where night and day would meet.

"I have been waiting for you. Come, I have much to show you…"

Cairo

Dinayra's headaches are worsening by the day. Night Herb will only do so much for a temporary amount of time, but ultimately there is nothing anyone can do...at least not yet. Closing the door behind me, I head towards her living room and take refuge on the sofa that is in dire need of replacement. I've offered many times to buy Dinayra a new couch, but she always refused, claiming that this sofa – which she affectionately named "Charles" – has sentimental value. No sooner than I plop down on the cushions, my phone buzzes for my attention. Reaching across the glass coffee table, an unknown number of flashes across my screen. But I do not need to see the number to know who is on the other line.

"Hello?"

"Cairo, how is everything?"

"Not so good..."

"Shit. Strange things are beginning to happen. Have you seen the news?"

"Not lately," I reach for the remote and turn on the tv. "What happened?"

"Well, a flock of birds apparently flew themselves into the propellers of a small plane in Oregon."

I sigh. "That's not a sure fire sign of pending death and doom Michael."

"There has been a series of earthquakes that struck Costa Rica, Honduras and Brazil within a three day span."

"Nothing but coincidence...not enough to indicate that someone has found the Book."

"If she is awakening Cairo, chances are someone has found the Book."

"She was going to awaken regardless. It's time. The thing is if no one reads from the text her full power cannot be activated."

"That's not what the others are saying," Michael protested. "She wasn't supposed to awaken for another thousand years- at least that was my understanding. If no one has accessed the book yet, then that means something, or *someone* has triggered her."

I pause. Who could that someone or something be? "If someone accessed that book Michael, you and I would both know."

"Someone has it Cairo. I can feel it. I've felt it throughout the ages, I just could not pinpoint its location. But I suspect it is a lot closer than we think. The vibrations of the earth have changed, and it won't be long before humanity feels it too. We don't have much time."

"I know, I know… but she isn't the only entity we have to worry about…Azrael."

"Fuck."

"My thoughts exactly."

"If she awakens, you know what you have to do," Michael says grimly.

"I know…"

"The rest of us will continue our search for the book and for Azrael. But Kalima cannot be allowed to enter this world."

Michael disconnects the call and leaves me to my thoughts.

"FUCK!" I cursed, throwing myself backwards against the couch. I watch her ceiling fan above me spin in a continuous slow cycle, lazily generating a small current of air that teases a few strands of my hair.

This is all completely fucked up. Dinayra doesn't deserve this. For months I've watched the headaches take a toll on Dinayra. Since the evening that I finally found the human vessel destined for Kalima to reawaken in, I have made it my point to never leave her side. Dinayra has yet to discover the fact that an ancient goddess – a goddess of destruction- lives within her and that she is a descendant of the people who once worshipped her. Now, it is only a matter of time before Kalima takes full control of Dinayra.

And I can't let that happen – not again.

I set my phone down on the coffee table and listened for

movement upstairs. The energy in the townhouse is still and after holding my breath for a few seconds too long, finally, I release an exhale. Dinayra is resting and hopefully by the time she wakes up, either Michael or one of the other Archangels will have word on the Book.

TWO

Dinayra

I found myself slipping through the void: plummeting through the dark spaces of infinite beginnings and endings until I crash landed in the center of an open field. I regard the lush greenery and the warmth of the sun with a vague familiarity, like I have been here before. Strange. My hands and knees ache from the collision, but I still push myself up to get a better view of my new surroundings. Off in the distance, I hear the low rumble of the tide. The salty scent of the sea floods my nostrils and I am instantly reminded of childhood when I would spend entire days at the beach.

Where am I?

From the corner of my eye, I notice a figure slowly approaching me from a short distance. Her thick locks were tightly coiled around her head like a crown. Her robing enhanced her already ethereal appearance: her rich dark skin juxtaposing the white fabric that clung tightly to her skin. As she advanced closer to me, I could tell that she stood no taller than I: 5'7", but where she lacked in height, she made up for in presence. With each step, it seemed as if each blade of grass parted to make room for her foot. Her dark eyes held the secret of her power, and it was through the same pair of eyes, I was able to look directly into the cosmos.

"I have been waiting for you," she told me, her voice as soft as the gentle wind that greeted us.

Everything about her felt familiar, especially her voice. I've heard her whisper to me from the dark spaces of my mind, after slipping into unconsciousness from the migraines. I used to hear her voice all the time when I was a child. She would reach out to me, coaxing me into a verbal embrace whenever my parents would argue and fight. She was there when I was bullied on the school grounds, offering to assist me in my school yard battles if I just agreed to setting her free. Free from what? I would often wonder. In my dreams I would see glimpses of her face, but now as she stood before me, staring face to face with the fullness of her beauty, for a moment I am paralyzed.

"Who are you?" I manage to say after a beat.

She inches closer until we are almost nose to nose, and she gently pushes a stray strand of hair away from my face.

"You are absolutely divine," she utters with a smile.

I should be saying the same thing about her, I think to myself.

"You are perfection," she continues with a smile. Her perfect white teeth are almost too much for me to look directly at. Everything about her is like gazing directly into the brightness of the sun.

"Where am I?" I stammer, taking a step back.

"You are within the boundaries of the Veil, the fabric of energy that separates everything from everything," she says. She then points in the direction where the land meets the sea. "Isn't it beautiful here?"

I follow her gaze and I have to admit that I am enjoying the peace and serenity of our surroundings. "It is. But I still don't understand... who are you?"

She looks at me, her smile brightens, and she reaches for my hair again, toying with the curly strands in her delicate fingers. "You will understand in time," she begins. "And Time has become scarce... Do you like it here?"

What an odd question, I think to myself. "It's beautiful here. It has been so long since I have been able to come to the beach...I didn't realize how much I've missed it."

"Good. I thought that you might like it. I want you to be at peace..."

I'm ready to wake up now. "Am I dreaming?"

"Yes and no. But I am as real as you are. Here..." she offers me her hand. "Touch me."

I accept her hand into mine and she is as warm as the grass underneath our feet. "I am very real," she tells me. "Just forgotten..."

"What do you mean? Who are you?" I demand quickly.

She looks away, her gaze focused on the skyline. "You've always known me little one," she began. "I have always been with you."

"I still don't understand," I say, searching around. The grass beneath us begins to fade. "What's happening?" The sound of the ocean slapping against the shoreline disappeared.

"You are returning to your world little one," she said grimly. "But you and I will see each other again. A new dawn is approaching, and I will rise as the new sun."

She reaches for my hand but instantly I slip away, and I find myself falling once again through the dark void of eternity. Her voice is still whispering to me, bringing me comfort as I continue to plummet until...

My eyes snap open and I sit up from the comfort of my bed. My room is dark and for a second, I could hear the voice of the mysterious entity who has been both my guardian and protector for all of my life. *"We will meet again soon little one,"* she whispered to me again. Little one, a name I would always go by when she spoke to me. How come I never recalled these memories until now? Out of habit I reached over for Cairo who would normally be sleeping soundly next to me in my bed, but tonight, his side remained empty.

Maybe he wanted me to have space to rest, I ponder as I slip out of the bed. The migraines had worsened over the course of the last few weeks and usually at night. He suffered just as much as I did, often staying up with me, making me tea and massaging my temples until whatever narcotic I took released its effects.

For now, the pain is gone and so is the nausea, and despite how late it might be, now is the perfect time to shower. I slide out of the bed and make my way to the bathroom and as soon as I cut the light on, I glance at myself in the mirror. Dark circles surrounded my almond shaped eyes. It seemed as if no matter how long I sleep, it is never enough.

"What is wrong with me?" I murmur to myself, looking into the mirror that hangs above the sink. The same question that I have asked myself again and again throughout the years remained unanswered. However, I had the sneaking suspicion that whatever answers I receive, I just may not be ready for what was to come.

CHAPTER

THREE

Cairo

I spent all night researching strange sightings and unexplained phenomenon that would indicate that the book had been found. For centuries I aided the Archangels in their quest to locate the Book of Obsidian to ensure that not a single page is opened. The first time Kalima awakened to her power, she wrought havoc on the cosmos. The planetary alignment was manipulated by her Scythe; it was like watching her rearrange the hands of a clock. The fact that she is one of the three most powerful entities ever created is both awe inspiring and terrifying...and should all three awaken at the same time, the world, the universe as we all know it is done.

She was birthed from the celestial body known as Saturn, which ultimately became her source of power, while the other planets throughout the Solar System had been simply given to the older Divinities both known and unknown to humanity. As a result, the movement of Saturn as it rotates around the sun has always revealed the next time Kalima will make her return. We had been watching the planet's movement for almost thirty years and it was thirty years ago when we discovered Saturn had aligned with Pluto and Neptune at the same time that Mars and Mercury had gone into retrograde. This could only mean one thing: Kalima had been reborn. But according to the Seraphim, the Keepers of Prophecy, it was said that instead of manifesting in her pure physical form, this time, she would secret herself away in another body. It was all just a matter of finding her human host.

And it also meant that we were running out of time to find that cursed book.

By the time I shut my computer off, it's after 7 a.m. and I can hear Dinayra upstairs shifting about. Last night was not as bad as the prior migraine episodes, which gave me hope that Kalima was too weak to fully take Dinayra over. And maybe, just maybe we can exist another lifetime without Kalima's destruction. The floorboards above me creak from Dinayra making her way downstairs. She trailed Dove and the soft scent of papaya as she carefully came down the stairs wearing her favorite purple robe and her hair wrapped tightly in a towel.

"Good morning," I say, trying not to sound exhausted.

"Good morning," she replied. She eyed me suspiciously and frowned. "Were you up all night again?"

"Yeah," I admitted. "I had some more work to do."

"It seems like I'm not the only one who needs some time off," she said as she hopped off the last step. "Want something to eat?"

"I should be asking you that," I say as I get up. "Those migraines don't seem to be getting any better..."

She looks at me and sighs. "You know, I've gone through worse periods than this."

"I'm sure you have, but I don't know... You sure you don't want to try to get another appointment with the neurologist?" A part of me just wants to confess to her that she has the spirit of an ancient and dark goddess living within her and that her "awakening" is

22

approaching. But then, another part of me wonders if she is already aware of what is happening to her. Has Kalima revealed herself to her in some way?

"No. I've been in and out of neurological labs for almost my entire life and no one could figure out what is wrong with me," she says without emotion. "It's just one of those things that I will have to live with."

But not for long, I think to myself. Soon, the fight for Dinayra to maintain control over her own will and body will be lost. My heart aches at the thought. It had been a long time since I've been in the company of a woman such as Dinayra. When I first met her, she held so much light in her eyes; her sense of humor and loving nature is what drew me towards her. But there is something else about Dinayra that I'm sure she doesn't know...

I observe her go into the kitchen and begin busying herself with pots and pans; and within a few minutes the house comes alive with the warm hearty scent of fresh Colombian coffee and bacon. I use this time to check the messages on my phone and one of them is from Gabriel.

Meet us at the Gallery at sundown, the message reads. *There is something you must know.*

Ok, is all I reply back with. It pains me to have to leave Dinayra for even a minute, but looking at her move back and forth in the kitchen, stuffing her face with a cream cheese bagel, I think it is safe to say that she will be fine...

For now.

"You want a bagel?" Dinayra called out, interrupting my thoughts.

"Yeah, sure love," I tell her. She flashes a warm smile and quickly redirects her focus to the bacon. Another thing I appreciate about Dinayra: she loves to cook for me. When we first began our courtship two years ago, she was excited to demonstrate her culinary skills. And being that I am a man with a healthy appetite, I was just as excited to allow her the floor. As I recline on the couch, the thick scent of bacon now a siren's song to my stomach, my thoughts drift to a time long erased from human consciousness. It is interesting to think that humans believe that their Bible, Koran, or even their Torah accurately sums up their religious history in few verses. Their feeble minds could never fathom how many earthly beginnings took place, long before the story of "Adam and Eve". If only they knew...

I stood on the riverbank just as I had done many an evening before, to watch the sun descend beneath the horizon perhaps headed towards adventures unknown. My people were retreating into their thatched roof dwellings after spending the day gathering what was left of the harvest and preparing for the next. I had recently been initiated into manhood, wherein after months of training, I captured and killed a wild panther. I wore its skin during the ceremony, marked my skin with its blood and its sharp tooth hung around my neck as a token of victory. By the next full moon, it was planned for me to marry a young female who too had barely come of age. Her beauty was like none other found in our village and her name was often the topic of envy amongst the women – married and unmarried. Raven dark hair that cascaded down her spine like free flowing silk; Bedouin shaped eyes that could stop the heart of any man who meets them; a heart shaped mouth and honey brown skin that would even capture the attention of the goddess of love herself.

The men of the village envied me for such a gift and a few of them even attempted to bribe her father with rare gifts of precious stones with the hope that they would be offered her hand in marriage instead of me. But her father had always admired me, even when I was young; and he had approached my father with the offer shortly after her birth. So, there I stood, my bare feet sinking into the muddy bank, silently enjoying the subtle warmth of the evening and contemplating life as a married man.

"Do you love her?" A soft, feminine voice interrupted my thoughts. I spun around to meet the intruder and there she stood in all of her splendor. Long dark locks dripped down below her waist, her white

robbing, a striking contrast against her dark skin, a manifestation of the balancing of both light and dark energies. Her midnight colored eyes revealed secrets of the heavens and I found myself seeking answers.

"I do not know what you mean," I said finally.

She regards me with a smile and her laugh reminded me of the sweet chattering of the river birds that come to greet those collecting water in the morning. "You are bound to marry a girl you care not for; would not die for and yet you are content."

"It is our way," I shrugged. "She is beautiful and will bear me strong heirs."

"But would you die for her?"

Her question left me stumped. My people were connected by blood, by the children we bore, by the language we spoke, by the gods we worshipped...I would lay down my life for Zira just as I would for any member of our tribe.

"Yes, I would," I answered after a beat. "Why do you ask?"

"Because since the development of Time, I have watched the energies of the Divine Feminine suffer at the hands of the Masculine – especially in the hands of a covenant such as marriage." She looks over in the direction of my village, her eyes scanning the cluster of mud brick dwellings. "Such beauty..." she whispered.

"Who are you?" I ask, my question redirecting her focus towards me.

"The Bringer of Mercy," she said evenly. "You ask as if you do not know what you are," she continued as she began to walk away.

"Wait! What do you mean?"

She stopped short just as she approached a thicket of bushes and turned around. "Call me by name when you are truly ready to learn what you are."

"What is your name then?" I call out as she begins to fade.

"Kalima..."

It would be seven days before the night of my marriage ceremony that Kalima and I would meet again. And to say that she had stolen my heart after a single conversation would be an understatement. She was the breath of fresh air that my soul needed; the new beginning that I had longed for; and the answer to my unspoken prayer. I knew exactly what she was the night she appeared to me on the riverbank. It was not until I stood with the Archangels at my flank, standing at the epicenter of the world's destruction when I realized who she was.

And now every time I look into Dinayra's eyes, it's like staring into the soul of a true reaper, the ultimate harbinger. I had hoped that Kalima would simply remain silent as she lived through Dinayra's experience as a human and that maybe through her eyes she would see humanity as precious as the power that she yields, rather another target for her destruction. But as Dinayra struggles to maintain control over her own body, whether we are ready for it or not, Kalima will awaken.

I really need to find that book.

CHAPTER

FOUR

Cairo

I stood outside atop the rooftop bar amongst a small crowd of humans, looking out at the city that seemed to stretch on for miles. The sun had barely begun its descent on the horizon and the first of the evening stars were scattered across the sky. Before I left, Dinayra was resting in the comfort of her bedroom, propped up against a multitude of pillows, binge watching Moesha on Netflix. As always, I left no indication that there was even a problem: I left a trail of kisses from her forehead to her mouth before I high tailed it out of her townhome, with barely enough time to make it to my meeting. I take a hard sip of the Rum and Coke mixture, allowing the mixture to make its slow burn down my throat before knocking the rest of it back. It's been a while since I was last able to enjoy a good drink.

"Did anyone tell you that drinking is a sin?"

I turned around to face Michael, dressed as if he was personally invited to a royal wedding: Tom Ford black suit, matching leather loafers and ironically, a gold cross that hung from his neck. His

29

thick mane of blonde hair was smoothed back in a single plait that he tucked underneath his collar. Gabriel rounded the corner, bypassing a series of empty tables. But instead of appearing as if he was about to set foot in Buckingham Palace, he looked like he had just walked off the set of the Matrix. Dark sunglasses covered his cleanly shaven face; a dark long coat hung from his shoulders, and he surveyed his surroundings suspiciously.

"Says who?" I asked with a smile.

"You crud," Michael quipped as he examined me. "Thank you for coming on what feels like short notice."

"How is she?" Gabriel asked after giving Michael a slight nod.

"Right now, it seems that the worst is over – for now," I inform him. "Kalima is still too weak to assume full control."

"How long do you think it will take before she awakens?" Gabriel pressed. "Saturn is moving toward conjunction with Neptune in the next few days. That also means that the Veil will be thinner, and we will not be able to fend off both Kalima and the other malicious beings that have been trapped on the other side."

"We've done it before," Michael stated evenly.

"But given the state of humanity, we need our comrades to maintain their focus on the humans – not so much battle," Gabriel argued. "This is the only way-"

"To maintain the balance," Michael grumbled. "I know."

"You know, I've been thinking," Gabriel began as he paced slowly from the chair to the balcony. "We have scoured the earth for ages looking for that book. Not a single clue has turned up that have pointed us even in its direction..."

"What are you saying?" I asked, frowning. My gut already does not like where this is going.

"When we sealed Kalima away the first time, we were too focused on ensuring that she could not escape than on locating her book and returning it to the seventh realm. Someone helped her hide the Book of Obsidian, perhaps one of her adoring worshippers."

"Again, what are you saying" I demand, placing my drink down on the nearby table.

"What I'm saying is, Kalima is the only one who knows where her book is. She knew that we would come for her, which prompted her to plan accordingly. I'm willing to bet that book is a lot closer than we think, masked by some sort of dark magic."

"Of course, she knows," I say, releasing a frustrated sigh. "Once she takes enough control over Dinayra to where she can access her book herself and unlock her full power, it will be another cosmic Genesis."

"That's not the only problem Cairo," Michael said grimly. "It is not our job to inform you of what takes place in the higher realms, but it is only fair that I inform you that our Reapers are becoming a little more rebellious. They can sense her power drawing near and will heed her call when the time comes."

"Ok," I say offering a hard stare at both archangels, more questions bombarding my mind. "I remember that scenario…"

"The Reapers are responsible for preventing Azrael from entering the earth realm. They protect the gateway of the Veil among other things. Azrael is responsible for converting Kalima's power into words and therefore shares a link to the book as well. He has been banished from the higher realms and denied access to the earth realm. If he finds and opens that book and calls Kalima forward, the two of them will undoubtedly destroy everything in the process of trying to annihilate each other. Azrael doesn't have Kalima's power; but he does have some control over the Book of Obsidian which may ultimately make him Kalima's puppet master."

"I will have to disagree," I mutter pointedly. "Azrael wants Kalima's power for himself. I've suspected that there is an even greater plan here. I just can't figure out what. Kalima has no use for Azrael. As a matter of fact, he is a sworn enemy of hers."

"You may have a point," Gabriel says pointedly. "But let's think about it, before, Kalima didn't need a human host and pretty soon, she won't. I know you care for Dinayra and…"

"I am not taking Dinayra's life if that is what you are thinking to put an end to Kalima," I hiss.

Gabriel's eyes widen and he looks at Michael for support. "I would never ask you to take Dinayra's life. That goes against Cosmic Law. Besides, even if Dinayra dies, Kalima would gain immediate control over the body."

The world suddenly feels heavy- too heavy for me to continue to carry. Michael offers a sympathetic look and then motions for me to have a seat at the empty table where my drink sat.

"It's a wonder that Kalima has yet to recognize you," Michael adds. "I thought from the moment you and Dinayra met, that would have immediately prompted her awakening."

"I don't think that Kalima and Dinayra are fully connected as of yet," I say, sounding defeated. "This is just a theory, but I don't believe that Kalima can have full dominion over Dinayra without her permission, at least not now anyway. If Dinayra concedes to Kalima, then I already know there will be immediate hell to pay."

"Sucks to be you," Gabriel said smugly.

"I think it's time you spoke to Dinayra about what is going to happen – and soon. For all we know, Kalima could have already been communicating with her."

"Dinayra may be able to provide you with some clues about where the book is; thus, allowing us to find it and make sure Kalima can never break free. And you and Dinayra could live out her human days with a happily ever after."

Even though the two of them were of the highest order of angels, it didn't ease the temptation to punch them in their smug faces.

"Look, I understand that being a Keeper is not an easy task," Michael said calmly. "But you have done well and believe that however this turns out is for the greater good."

"Are we done here?" I reach my drink and gulp the rest of it down and slam the glass down hard on the table. The two angels look at me and shake their heads. "What?"

"Yeah, we are done," Michael sighs. "Keep us updated. And Cairo?"

"What?"

"This isn't easy for any of us either," Michael stated plainly. "We know Dinayra is a good soul, and we are doing everything we can do to try to save her."

My gaze bounces between Michael and Gabriel. As much as I wanted to trust and believe in them as Archangels, the highest ranking beings next to the Seraphim in the heavenly realms, I can't. I already know how this will end. They must have forgotten that I was there when Kalima decided to wield her Scythe. It took damn near the entire company of heaven to stop her.

There is nothing more for me to say to either of them. I turned to walk away, quickly bypassing the bar and a few patrons that had just arrived. Images of Dinayra's beautiful face filter in through my mind's eye. She has suffered for far too long; her body not strong enough to continue a fight between a human soul and the powerful spirit of a goddess.

I'm so sorry D, I think to myself as I step foot into the elevator. Perhaps my dealings with Kalima in the past is what set the tone for my karma here in the present. Maybe, just maybe all of this is really my fault. And if this is true, the fact of the matter is, I am not the only one paying for it.

FIVE

Dinayra

I t's been months since I can recall what it means to experience peace within myself; meaning, for years it felt like I have been fighting a losing battle for dominance over my own mind. My childhood is plagued with memories of sitting in a therapist's chair, meeting the curious stare of whatever licensed family therapist was assigned to my case while trying to explain the voice in my head. At first, my parents had written it off to me just going through a phase of having an imaginary friend. However, as time went on, the voice that would slip into my consciousness occasionally went from being a subtle, almost invisible presence to a loud- speaker. In time I realized that whoever this female apparition was, she was seeing the world through my eyes and wanted answers to questions that I could not answer during my childhood. And there are still many things I cannot answer as an adult.

For whatever reason, it seems that my "companion" has disappeared for the time being and thankfully, she took the migraines with her. For now, I can truly think without interruption. And it is a bit strange to admit that as I sit here, staring at the flat screen mounted on my wall, there is a void. Her absence reminds me that as a thirty three year old adult in this world, I am truly alone. True enough, Cairo has been with me for some time now, but there are moments when I wonder when he will tire of my sleepless nights and hard mornings and trips to the emergency room and leave? He is a good man and deserving of a life with a normal, healthy woman.

But yet, he stays. He acts as if he is my personal guardian, making sure that should I stumble, I don't fall. He watches me as if he is expecting something to happen – as if he knows something. It's always in his eyes; his whiskey brown stare filled with both concern and horror. I don't know if he believes that one of these days, he is going happen upon my unresponsive body and...

I shrug off the thought.

Instead of plunging into dark thoughts, I refocus my attention on cartoon image of a young boy and girl who realize that the orphanage that they have been living in is a human farm for demons. I lose myself in the plot, drifting off to sleep sometime after the "Mom" eyes one of the older children with suspicion. It isn't long before I am back standing barefoot near the seashore. The hard caw of the seagull echoed overhead, and the warmth of the sun felt too good for me not to tilt my head back to embrace the gentle heat.

"I see you have returned," the female says as she took form in front of me. "I knew you would."

I look around before my gaze finally meets her dark eyes. "How do I even get here?" I ask.

"We are connected, you and I."

"Who are you?"

"Someone the world has forgotten long ago," she begins. "But the time has come for me to return." She pauses before continuing. "My

name is Kalima. I am the keeper of Time, a Harvester and Dominion over the Reapers. I am what the world needs to reset balance and order."

I consider her words for a moment. I've read about beings in mythology, beings responsible for the reshaping and shaping of worlds; creators of universes; destroyers of time and space... This cannot be real, I think to myself.

"Oh, but what is reality?" Kalima asks me. "Is it only what you are able to see, taste, smell, touch...? Can you not see me? Can you not feel the grass beneath your feet?"

Without thinking, I wiggle my toes against the grass. She has a point.

"Reality is what we make of it regardless; if you are human, spirit or god," she adds. "There are those destined to play a role in the matrix created by others, never being able to set foot outside of the invisible prison that contains them. And then, there are those who are destined to wield it...and then there are others like myself who are here to put an end to it."

"Why am I here?" I ask softly, intuitively I begin to understand who she is. I have felt her energy, her presence, her darkness for as long as I could remember.

"Because we are one...because you are the only one who will understand my purpose," Kalima began evenly. "I have watched you live in your world through your eyes...I have seen every cause of your disappointments and your pain. I have felt your joys, heard your laughter, loved those you loved...Your anger was mine as was your pleasure, Dinayra. All who have wronged you, all who have wronged the innocent, misled the blind, damaged the souls of the weak... will meet the end of my Scythe."

So, humanity doesn't have a choice? Fear creeps into my spirit and I take a step back. All right, it's time to wake up now, I think to myself.

"You have no reason to fear me," she says. "I will not harm you."

"I hate to break it to you, but it sounds like destroying the world is a part of your plan and I happen to reside in that world."

"I have ways of keeping those I love safe," Kalima breathed. *"You would be safe."*

"And then what? I return to a world where there is no one but me in it?"

She ignores my question and sighs. *"One way or another Dinayra, what is to come will come. It is prophecy. There are those in the higher realms that are looking for me as I speak. They are aware of my pending arrival."*

"Why are you telling me this?" I whisper, searching her face for answers.

"Because they will be looking for you too. If I am going to protect you Dinayra, set me free..."

Dinayra...

"Release me Dinayra..."

Dinayra!

My eyes snap open and I see Cairo looking down at me, his expression grim. His five o' clock shadow had returned with a vengeance and instantly I wondered if he had gone another night without sleep. He is breathing heavily, his collared shirt unbuttoned revealing his tattooed pectorals and his neatly tied locks had come undone.

"What's wrong?" I ask groggily. "What happened?"

Cairo leans forward and gently places a kiss on my forehead. His gaze leads me to the direction of my window where a small group of ravens sat, staring into the glass.

"What the hell? Why are there a bunch of birds sitting on my windowsill?" I blurt out.

"Dinayra," Cairo begins evenly. "We have to talk."

CHAPTER
SIX

Cairo

I tiptoed into the house, just to be greeted by the warmth from the wall heater, which instantly soothed the anxiety that crept up within me soon after the meeting with the two Archangels. At least now I have a little more time to mentally prepare for the conversation that will definitely change the scope of our relationship. Or worse... My heart aches from the burden of having to reveal to the woman that I love the danger of who she is and what is anticipated to come. As I begin my slow and reluctant ascension up the stairs, the weariness from my soul makes each step feel like a challenge. I have waited for a millennium, watching, and preparing for the moment that Kalima's spirit awakens. And as the day draws nigh, I still have yet to get my hands on the book that will activate the power of her Scythe.

Memories from a life that history never recorded flooded my mind as I approached Dinayra's bedroom. Dark orbs filter in and out of her bedroom which give me pause while Dinayra slept peacefully to the sound of the television quietly playing in the backdrop. I swallow thickly and contemplate making a call to Michael. The last thing I want to do is deal with Reapers who are now acting as guardians over Dinayra's sleeping form.

"Fuck," I whisper as I cross the threshold. At least a dozen dark orbs surround me like a viral army set on attacking the body's natural defense system. I furiously attempt to bat them away, but my hands just slip right through their transparent forms. The last time I had to encounter a group of Reapers was when Kalima had come into full power, and she summoned them to aid her in her fight against their brethren. Black winged entities armed with sickles instead of scythes like their leader – the Grim Reaper – swooped upward to meet Michael and the other Archangels midair. I remember Gabriel tossing me a specially made blade handed down directly from the Seraphim just so that I could stand a chance in battle.

This was not a good sign at all.

"Get away from me you little creeps!" I hiss. "She will not awaken – not now, not ever!"

"Says the one who betrayed her," they all squealed in unison. "Her wrath will be like a thousand storms, a thousand flames, and a thousand deaths."

"I had no choice," I grumbled. "I gave Kalima my heart once and she nearly damned my soul."

"This world sits on a pendulum that swings toward its own destruction," they continued. "The cries of the wounded, the broken and the damned have reached her ears. Archangels have done nothing, and humanity now sits on the brink of collapse. The damned rule the weak and that is not the way. The damned have tampered with the Veil and summon dark energies that they can no longer contain and soon, another entity far older than Kalima will awaken."

"Who then? If Kalima awakens, the world will end," I whisper.

"If Kalima does not awaken, both worlds of spirit and flesh will be condemned to eternal death. The world and the realms in between are in need of a rebirth. Ye, who spilled her blood on the mountain top; ye who promised you fealty to her...How do you consider yourself a Keeper when you know nothing about the prophecy..."

"I know what I have done," I say quickly. "And I have read many texts about the prophecy of Kalima's Scythe and the destruction that is to follow."

"You of all people should know that Kalima is neither good nor evil. She exists to assist with a cleanse-"

"It only speaks of her wrath. Kalima will summon forth two ancient beings who have remained hidden away in the cosmos. And together they will form a Trinity of Vengeance...She is the key to unleashing the Four Horsemen."

"The Four Horsemen already travel the skies but are not in this world at this time. But if you listen closely, you may still hear the sound of their horses' feet strike the air like thunder. And her wrath is for the unjust. The unjust souls will be contained in her world where they will face judgement. Those whose hearts do not call for the Reaping from her Scythe will be reborn in new world without bloodshed, war, and pain."

"I will not argue with the lot of you any longer," I declare. "You serve the ultimate goddess of death!"

"A debt and a score must be settled before the Cleanse. Gods far older than you Cairo will return. It was in Kalima's vision which is why she called for her Scythe." The orbs began to fade but not before concluding with, "Be not a fool Cairo. The old Ones are coming... ask Uriel."

And almost instantly, the dark orbs disappear.

I glance over at Dinayra who is mumbling and uttering something unintelligible from the bed. Her eyes snap open, bright white light consuming her irises.

"Dinayra!" I call out as I rush toward her. "Dinayra!" I reach for her and gently shake her, hoping that it will be Dinayra who responds and not Kalima.

She slips back into unconsciousness and panic begins to take a stronghold as I shake her a little harder. The slow rise and fall of her chest are a good sign, but the fact that she hasn't woken up despite my attempts is still unnerving.

I call her name again and again and then finally; she opens her eyes. A disoriented but normal brown eyed gaze looked up at me. I release a sigh of relief and scoot over to make room for her to sit up. A hard pecking on her glass window captured both of our attentions. Kalima's chosen bird, the raven had landed on her windowsill. But as soon as its feet landed, several others joined it: each one staring directly at her through the window.

I wished there could have been a better way for me to ease her into the conversation that needed to be had but there was no time. I met her confused gaze and said quickly, " Dinayra, we have to talk."

SEVEN

Dinayra

I don't know which is worse: losing the fabric of reality that Fate had constructed as my life; or realizing that the life that I believed belonged to me wasn't mine at all. I've been existing as a pawn for a game far bigger than what I could fully comprehend. But what I did not expect was Cairo's role in it. He could hardly look at me as he fumbled with his words to explain what I had been experiencing and grown to know all along.

"She has been coming to me since I was young," I began. "Making appearances here and there...my parents thought I was crazy and signed me up for therapy."

"I can imagine how tough that was for you," Cairo said evenly. "They had no way of knowing or understanding..."

"I guess they wouldn't... I can picture the discussion going something like this: 'hey mom, dad, I have an ancient goddess of death living inside me. But don't worry, she is just going to unleash hell fire into the world to save it...' Yeah, I can see that conversation." I pause and look down at my trembling hands. So much was said over the last forty minutes and there is too much to take in. However, it's still difficult for me to digest the fact that the man that has been by my side for the last couple of years knows more about me than I do. "Question," I say after a deep breath. "You said that you know Kalima. How?"

He looks away, his gaze fixed on the ceiling. His thick locks came undone and spilled out over the pillowcase. Dark circles had begun to form around his almond shaped eyes and his normally cleanly shaven face was in need of a touch up.

"I'm a lot older than you can imagine Dinayra," He breathes. "Truthfully, I never wanted to have to tell you any of this... I wanted to experience a full human life with you."

"Full human life?" I repeated. What does he mean by that?

"Dinayra, I am what you would consider to be an immortal. There are only a few of us left in the world. I came from a tribe of people who were descendants of those considered to be Atlanteans. We were destined to be Keepers of scrolls and other ancient texts...but, as always things happened."

"Atlanteans? Like as in 'the lost city of Atlantis?'"

He chuckles and gently rubs his palm over my cheek. "Yes, you are correct."

If it wasn't for my own experiences: the feelings, the sensations; the visions... I have touched her, heard her voice... I've been to a world that does not exist in this one...Cairo revealing that he is an immortal isn't as laughable as one would expect. If anything, it is a relief. At least someone has knowledge of what I am dealing with.

"Only those who were there before the first beginning possess knowledge of Kalima," Cairo murmured. "That's why her name was never found in temples or scrolls even. True enough there are entities that mimicked her likeness, but none would ever be as powerful."

"But who was she to you?" I pressed. A part of me had already known the answer. It was the way his eyes continued to stare blankly at the ceiling; the slight crinkle of his nose and the tension in his face as he fought hard not to smile. Jealousy tugged at my heart strings, but I take in a deep breath and try to ignore the feeling. As if sensing my discomfort, he reaches over and slides his hand down my back and pulls me in closer.

"She was the very first breath I took when my eyes opened in the morning; she was my heartbeat and my soul...at the time, she was my everything."

Damn. Another pang in my heart reawakens old wounds from past heartbreaks that were nothing more than one sided relationships that left me emotionally bankrupt. Is that why he is with me? He knows that at some point he will reunite with *her?* Is that what he has been waiting for this entire time? I keep my thoughts to myself and force myself to listen. The truth always carries a painful sting for someone who isn't ready to hear it. Perhaps, I believed too strongly that Cairo was a fairytale come true and that indeed our relationship is exactly that: a fairytale.

As he spoke, I thought about all four of my past relationships where I convinced that the man I loved was "the one" – with Cairo being the fourth. And in reality, they were "the one" for someone else; meanwhile, it seems as if Fate has other plans for me. I guess the real question I should be asking is why me?

EIGHT

Cairo

It had been nearly seven days before Kalima returned to my village. Her appearance had caused quite a stir as children had joyfully surrounded her, encouraging her to engage with them in song. I spotted her from the corner of my eye while my soon to be father in law discussed the building of a new temple wherein our recently acquired "Underwater Scrolls" might be kept. It wasn't required of my people to pay homage to the gods; that responsibility belonged to the increasing populations of humans that had yet to evolve, however, it was not uncommon for a divine being to appear and interact with any member of the village. But it quickly became quite clear that Kalima was no ordinary being.

I watched as she smiled and took the hands of two young females and danced about in a circle, laughing, and singing. Her smile was as radiant as the moon on a clear night. Her long braid swung against her waist and this time, instead of white robing, she donned black fabric that first wrapped around her waist with a deep split that exposed the fullness of *her long legs. The same fabric was wrapped tightly around her breasts and from her neck hung a glassy black gem that proudly guarded her heart. Her locks were piled up on top of her head like a crown. Bracelets made of seashells wrapped around her wrists and ankles. For a moment, time stopped, and it seemed as if the entire village were enchanted by the magic that was Kalima.*

She glanced over in my direction and smiled as she continued to dance with the children. For a second or perhaps for even a half of century – time did not exist whenever our eyes would meet – she took me on a journey through the cosmos, to where the higher deities sat above the universe and mapped out the stars. She took me to the very space of creation where I witnessed infinite possibilities of the past, present and future. The urge to join her in singsong, to hold her hand and dance with the children was nearly too much; but the heated gaze from my future wife and her father snapped me out of the daydream and brought me right back into the present.

"It seems that you have captured the attention of a Dingir," Harab, my soon to be father in law stated evenly. "I am unsure if her visit here is a good sign or if this is a sign of pending doom."

"Don't you think that if she wanted to destroy our village she would have?" I asked, looking back at Kalima who was still enjoying herself dancing with the children.

"You are the next Keeper Asir," Harab told me. "I promised your father that I would pass of my knowledge of the Ancients to you so that you may act as a bridge between those who walk in Spirit; those who wield the powers of the universe; those who sit High in judgement; those who lurk within the darker realms and those who walk in the flesh. While your father continues to guard the Gates, it is my responsibility to ensure that you are prepared to carry the Light and to act as both your father and I have as a Torch Light of Knowledge. We protect the secrets of the gods and prepare the prophecies. But no matter how tempting, we must not submit to the seduction of the lords and madams of the other realms..."

"I have not submitted to anything," I grumble.

Harab followed my gaze and rested his eyes on Kalima. "From the looks of it, you may not have a choice..."

"What do you mean he doesn't have a choice father?" Zira snaps, instantly capturing the attention of both her father and me. "What would look like for me as a wife if my husband were ensnared in the arms of a Dingir?!"

She looks at me, her beautiful Bedouin eyes silently pleading with me for reason. I knew Zira had genuine feelings for me; perhaps more than I had for her. She was the ideal wife; she was the vision of every available bachelor in our village. Soft spoken, kind, beautiful, knowledgeable in many things which made conversing with her easier... But even as she silently demanded that I remain faithful to my pledge to her, my thoughts still drifted to Kalima.

Harab looked at me and sighed. "The wedding will still commence as planned. But as the current Keeper, I do need to find out what she wants and how we are best able to serve her. I have never seen her before and there is no record of her...this concerns me."

Zira frowns and marches off silently, in the direction of the home she shares with her family. Harab's gaze offers a bit of sympathy which then deepens my guilt. It was never my intention to hurt Zira in any way. But then I hear Kalima's voice filter into my consciousness like a gentle whisper, "But would you die for her?"

As I continued to watch Kalima uplift the children with her presence, I soon realized that the answer to her question regarding my love for Zira was no.

I wasn't sure how Dinayra felt after my brief disclosure of a memory from long ago. This was only the beginning; the beginning to what may very well be the end. Dinayra said nothing as she continued to nervously play with her hair. She had looked away when I spoke of Zira, but she grew tense as I dove into the beginning chemistry, I had with Kalima. I wonder if she too will grow to hate me as I'm sure Kalima had when I was had to plunge my blade into Kalima's chest and cast her away, back into the protective barrier of The Veil.

But with Dinayra… this is different. It's like reliving the memories with Kalima all over again while having to contend with this new painful reality of losing a woman that I love. After Kalima, there were a few others that I had grown to cherish but thanks to the inequities of Time, the relationships ended almost as quickly as they began.

"I think you should go, Cairo," she murmurs, pushing herself away from me.

"Wait, huh?" I ask, feeling completely confused. "I never wanted to hurt you."

She sighed. "I'm so tired of just…everything…"

"What do you mean? Talk to me," I take her wrist, but she gently eases it from my grip.

"All this time I thought I just… I don't know… was communicating with a ghost or something. A spirit. My parents thought I was crazy and were literally one phone call away from calling an exorcist. It's bad enough that I have had to deal with the massive migraines and doctors never able to pinpoint the cause of them- which now it makes sense why…" She turned around to wipe her face. My heart ached at the sight of a single tear that dripped from her palm and into her lap. "There has never been anything *normal* or *real* about me."

"Dinayra that's not true," I plead. "I understand that you have suffered-"

"Nothing," she continued as her voice began to tremble. "After all the heartaches and heartbreaks and not to mention the headaches, I thought that I had found something genuine.

54

Someone who was sincere and honest with his intentions towards me..."

"Wait, no D... just listen for a minute..."

"And all this time, you knew..."

"Dinayra-"

She shook her head and continued to avoid my gaze. "At this point, I don't know what to think. I just know that I have been in the presence of a man who is destined to live forever and even if I wasn't possessed by a goddess of death, every day I wake up is one day closer to my grave."

"Dinayra, I do love you, really..."

That caught her attention. She slowly turned to face me; unshed tears shimmered underneath the low light of her room.

"We have been together all this time and the fact that you decide to tell me this now tells me that you don't. You are here because you know Kalima is coming." She swallows thickly. "I don't know what your purpose is or your reasons for staying as close to me as you have but for the time that I have left, I just would like to be alone."

Her truth hurt me about as much as it did for her to say it. I had been so focused on preparing for Kalima and locating the book that I had failed her in one way too many. I never told Dinayra how I felt. I told her everything else except for what mattered and as I sit across from her, neither of us sure how much longer it will be before what may be the end... The words that she needs to not just hear, but accept fully as truth, could have been the strength that she needs to fight harder. And what's worse is, I never told Dinayra about who she is or took the time to prepare for this single moment.

"I understand I hurt you Dinayra and I can't take that back," I begin as I push myself off the bed. "I will give you the space that you need to figure things out."

She sat with her arms folded against her chest, tears raining from her face and onto her lap. I've never seen her like this. I just wanted to pull her into my arms and hold her there forever. But instead, I slowly kneeled before her and took her hands into my own.

"If you don't know anything Dinayra," I tell her with all sincerity. "Know that what I feel for you is real. I'm sorry that I never told you this before; but I do. I love you Dinayra and I don't want to lose you. Not to life, not to death and not to Kalima." I kiss her on top of her forehead and gently pull away. "I will give you some space, but I am never going to leave you alone."

It took everything in me to not pull her into my arms and kiss away her tears. But her silence is what begged me to continue my way out the door. I took my time heading down her stairs, hoping that she will change her mind.

She doesn't and to be honest, I can't blame her. My phone begins to buzz in my pocket; and I yank it out to answer just as I open the door. It's Michael.

"What's up?" I ask, stepping outside into the darkness. There was still a few hours left before the sun would reintroduce itself to the world. My footsteps echoed across the yard and far out into the street as I made my way to my car.

"We had to send reinforcements to cover The Veil; the Reapers are scouring the planet in search of the Book."

"Yeah…I just had a run in with some reapers myself…" I begin.

"What do you mean?" Michael asked, sounding alarmed.

"They were guarding her when I returned. Dinayra was sleeping – pretty much unconscious – when I found them in her room."

"That is a problem," Michael muttered. "That means that they know it is almost time. They might also know where the book is…"

"I also spoke with Dinayra," I unlock the door to my car and slide in.

"Oh. And I assume that didn't go too well," Michael replied. "What happened?"

"She is conscious of Kalima and always has been. Kalima has been communicating with her since she was a child. The thing is, I don't know exactly what Kalima has showed her, however Dinayra knows that she is running out of time..."

"I see. If we can retrieve that book before Saturn goes into retrograde – which is in three days to be exact – then we might have a chance at saving her. Are you with Dinayra now?"

"No. I am leaving her house as a matter of fact."

"That bad huh?"

"Yeah..."

"Gabriel is on his way with a few others to keep watch over her house," Michael confessed. "She won't know that they are there..."

Without thinking I release a sigh of relief. "She needed some space from me. I really hurt her..."

This time it was Michael who sighed. "She has a good soul and understands on some level that it was never your intent. Right now, she is only looking at the situation through lenses of hurt. She feels alone but, in enough time - "

"Which she doesn't have," I add grimly.

"Oh, ye of little faith," Michael contended. "She will be ok. Everything is always for a higher purpose."

Before I turn my key into the ignition, my thoughts return to the whispers of caution that came from the Reapers. Michael is a little too focused on obtaining the Book of Obsidian while there just might be another entity out there that only Kalima is strong enough to destroy. Here I am again, sitting on the precipice of having to make a choice between Kalima or death.

"You're right," I say finally. "I'm going to head home and get a few hours rest. I will check on Dinayra later on."

"Good, you're going to need it. I will check in with you soon."

After disconnecting the call, I felt the weight of a thousand years of fatigue. I muster the strength that I have left and pull off. The last thing I want to do is further upset Dinayra if she happens to still see my car parked out front of her house. A few hours away will give me the time I need to think and find out more about Neptune. Michael and Gabriel have their secrets, but one thing about being a Keeper is that I also have mine.

Azrael

"The time has come my lord," Aralkyl stated cautiously as he approached. His heavy footsteps echoed throughout the hallway of the temple, nestled at the very center of one of the largest celestial bodies near Orion's belt.

"I can feel her dark energy growing stronger by the day," Azrael grumbled as he approached the massive tomb. "Have you found the book?"

"I can detect its presence somewhere near Kalima's incarnated form," Aralkyl admitted. "The Reapers are working diligently to locate it."

"I see...have you tried making contact with the girl? She might have some clue as to where the book is being kept." Azrael pressed. He glanced at the metal slab where he kept his arsenal of weapons and grabbed a trident and examined the pointed ends.

"No. Michael and Gabriel are watching over her among others... Asir has even reinserted himself as her mate," Azrael confessed.

"Hm that does complicate things," Azrael grumbled, still examining the trident. His iridescent eyes regarded the weapon carefully. "The Veil is not thin enough just yet for me to push through..."

"We are working on it," Azrael said quickly. "Human scientists are being fed information daily on quantum mechanics and physics that have pushed them into running tests...we have spoon fed them information on what they consider to be extraterrestrial life which has furthered their curiosity to that beyond the earth and slowly their technology has worked wonders to pave the way for your return my lord."

"In three days', time, when Saturn goes into retrograde and falls into an alignment with Mars, Jupiter and Neptune, Kalima will reach full strength to summon her Scythe. We have to move quickly in order to make sure she does not Reap the Harvest. Michael and his band of bandits got in the way the last time..."

"Yes," Azrael agreed nervously. "We will not fail."

"You have twenty- four hours to grab that book...Neptune grows impatient by the hour. It will be another millennia before we are able to snatch another opportunity like this. It is time for the old gods to get their just due."

"Yes," Azrael said backing away. "I'm on it."

"Excellent."

Cairo's absence wraps around me like a cold gust of wind; I ache for the warmth of his presence; for his voice; for his laughter; for his touch... But knowing the full truth of his reasons for entering my life in the first place is a hard punch to the gut. An emotional pang to the chest triggers another round of tears. I bury my face in my hands and release a hard sob. Pain, heartache, disappointment, loss...those all seem to be common themes in my life. The constant migraines prevented me from having too much of a social life; and the ongoing sense of overwhelming dread would haunt me during most of my waking hours.

Intuitively, I knew that there was more to all of this; however, never would I have guessed that the voice and the visions were the promise of the return of an actual goddess. Growing up I fancied her to be something like a 'fairy godmother" or my personal protector. But now, I understand that I am nothing more than a vessel for an age old agenda that began probably not long after the creation and formation of the earth itself.

"Fear not child," her voice instantly captures my attention. *"I will cause you no harm."*

Quickly, I wipe my tears and look around. "What do you want?" I demand. "I can't even have a moment to myself-"

"I understand your pain. We are connected Dinayra...I know your pain as intimately as I know my own...And I know Cairo..."

I cringe at the mention of his name. A sharp pang of jealousy shoots through me and instantly my eyes are no longer filled with tears.

"Cairo's love for me died long ago," her voice is almost a whisper. *"He is the reason why I have been locked away here."*

"So, what do you want? Revenge?" I hear myself ask aloud. This is absolutely crazy. I am alone sitting on my bed talking aloud to a voice that only I can hear. Moments like this always took me back to my childhood when my mother would scold me for "talking to myself".

"I am far more evolved than a need for simple revenge," she said evenly. *"My purpose is not to wield the hand of vengeance against petty offenses. But I have silently observed your engagements with Cairo, hoping that he would one day he would understand what was supposed to happen eons ago, would not be prevented."*

"And what was supposed to happen?" A part of me does not want to know the answer. I'm too mentally and emotionally exhausted to continue talks of the pending apocalypse – the same apocalypse brought on by an ancient goddess who has chosen me as her vessel.

"He is known by the Divine Masters as Neptune, but he has many other names," Kalima recounts. *"He is often mistaken for a lesser, ocean god – Poseidon- but that is inaccurate. He is far older than creation and at one point sat at the High Table, equal to that of the Seraphim. He sought to build his own world and recruited a number of angels to serve him and when man came...the fight for dominion over rights to the human spirit began."*

"So, what do I have to do with any of this?" I demanded, finally.

"Dinayra, all of your questions will be answered if you do one thing for me," Kalima offered.

Of course...why wouldn't an ancient goddess of death have a request of me, despite the fact that she has completely taken over my life. I release a slow exhale and throw myself backwards against the mattress. At this point, I am willing to do whatever to give myself more time to just be... me.

"What do you want me to do?"

"I need for you to claim what is mine: The Book of Obsidian."

I pause and shake my head. The Book of Obsidian? Why does that sound vaguely familiar?

"I know exactly where it is being kept," she says quickly. *"But you must retrieve it."*

"Ok...but why the rush?"

"There are others who are seeking out what is mine."

But what would happen if Kalima got ahold of her book though...I wonder. What would that mean for the rest of the world?

"It would mean that those who seek to destroy the world would not be able to do so," Kalima replied quickly. *"But before you do, let me show you something..."*

CHAPTER

TEN

Cairo

I 've spent so much time at Dinayra's house that it feels like ages since I last stepped across my own threshold. Fatigue eats away at me; while the weight of the world sits proudly on my shoulders, making it difficult to even focus. I spent centuries anticipating the day that all of this would end. I would locate the book, hand it over to Michael and Kalima's return would be a long forgotten memory. But now all I can think about is Dinayra. I cursed myself for being so mission focused; so, driven to prevent Kalima's return that ultimately, I failed her. At this point, she might not ever trust me again and to be honest, I wouldn't blame her.

It feels odd standing in the empty hallway of my own home. Egyptian relics line my hallway; carvings from the days of Mesopotamia that any world renowned archaeologist would love to get their hands on hang on my walls and rest on my coffee table. Babylonian texts are kept in the temperature controlled trunks that I keep locked away in one of my guest rooms. My house holds all of the mysteries of a museum and if it weren't for my own private security system, I would remain in constant worry over the protection of my countless artifacts. But thankfully, ADT has me covered.

Slipping off my shoes becomes a simple joy; and in no time, I'm wearing nothing but my Calvin Klein's. I bypass my almost life sized figure of Bastet and for a second, my mind ventures back to the days before The Veil had been lifted and the gods of the other realms walked among men. I remember the days before men thought of themselves as the gods they once worshipped. And now, here I am in a world where men believe in nothing but themselves...they no longer see the god within them, the God above them, let alone the gods that still walk among them.

Humanity has lost its sight and I wonder if that is why Kalima sought the power of her Scythe to end the world...to end the world before the world ended itself.

I don't even bother flipping the light switch on in my room. The peaceful reprieve of darkness is what I need to succumb to the pending the slumber. It is a strange feeling to slip between the softness of my silk sheets without the warm presence of Dinayra. I often found peace in listening to her soft snores as she slept soundly next me, a tangled mess in the blankets, but nonetheless a woman I had come to value more than life and that book itself.

"Be not a fool Cairo. The old Ones are coming... ask Uriel." The words of the Reapers return to me as I begin to drift. The image of Kalima's massive Scythe filters into my mind's eye. I recall hearing the whispers of The Old Ones echoing from the stars many a night, soon after I stepped into my role as a Keeper. But when Kalima began to wage war with the heavens, her cry for battle drowned out the hushed murmurs of old power.

What did Kalima know that even the Archangels did not?

I slip into unconsciousness before I attempt to mentally answer the question.

The women in the village welcomed Kalima with smiles and excitement –
with the exception of Zira. They escorted her to our temple where all of
our relics, scrolls and offerings to the various deities were kept. Built long
before my birth, shortly after the first breach of the earth realm. Built
with the purpose of being within Heaven's reach, the giant monolith
surpassed the tallest of trees and spread out across the terrain for several
hundred cubic feet. The triangular form of the building aligned with the
position of the star Sirius – the gatekeeper to that of which known as the
Underworld. The purpose of the temple was to act as a bridge between the
physical realm and that of which that is beyond it. The Keepers – those
who were chosen by The Watchers – to protect the sacred texts of the
temple; to keep records of cosmic events and the actions set forth by the
gods of man; and to essentially act as guardians for The Veil. Only a few
of us in my village were chosen; my father, his father; Harab; and myself.

I did what I could to keep a quiet distance from Kalima, but I could
still sense her searching for me. Even when I acted as Zira's private escort
from one end of the village to the next, there was no escaping the grip of
Kalima's power. Zira's family had already begun the preparations for our
"binding of the souls" ceremony – which is the equivalent of a wedding.
The more time I spent with Zira, the more I found my thoughts drifting
back to Kalima. Harab remained steadfast in his determination to find
out Kalima's identity and returned to the temple where he met with her
frequently; asking her questions about her power; her preference for
worship and what exactly drew her to the earth realm. However, by the
end of the third day of Kalima's presence in the temple, Harab sought a
petition to speak with The Watchers.

And after Harab lit the fire in the sacred bowl made of precious
metals, he placed the handwritten scroll into the flame and allowed the
embers to carry away the message. Meanwhile, Kalima no longer found
amusement from the support and adoration of the temple scribes or the
female worshippers who were called upon for assistance. Instead, she took

leave and wondered her way back to the village where she and I met again. This time, I was seated outside of the home I shared with my mother and my aunts, gazing up at the sky lost in my own remorse. Zira and I were not speaking again for the third time since Kalima's arrival. I had given her the choice to not go through with the Binding of Souls ceremony, but she refused and told me that doing so would bring dishonor to her family.

Harab would never forgive me for not moving forward with the marriage to his daughter. My father had promised him that our families would become one to ensure and strengthen the legacy of the Keepers bloodline. But as I looked up at the sky, admiring the infinite glory of the stars that hung above and all that transcended the beyond, Kalima appeared right beside me.

"You have been avoiding me Asir," she said, folding her arms across her chest.

I didn't look away from the sky to meet her probing stare. "I have... and for that I am sorry."

"Duty can be a curse. That female of yours refuses to acknowledge me or my power," she continued.

"She believes you are the reason for my lack of enthusiasm for marrying her," I answered quickly.

Kalima paused and looked in the direction of where Zira and her family rested. "I've seen her a few times from behind The Veil whenever I was curious to learn about the earth realm. She resents her position and lack of ability to be chosen as a Keeper. Are women not allowed such a position?"

Her question forced me to turn away from the sky and finally look at Kalima. Her dark skin nearly blended in with the night. The light from her eyes and her smile was what stood out from the darkness. "Long ago, yes."

She frowned and for a second, it felt strange knowing that I could sense her emotion just as deeply as my own. "An imbalance occurred between the masculine and feminine energies...that balance must be restored," she murmured to herself.

"Zira deserves so much more than what I could give her," I confessed without thinking. "There are other men in the village that would love for her to bear their heirs; to be overpowered by the softness of her touch and be influenced by her voice."

"And you desire none of it?" Kalima asked evenly.

"I am bound by my role as a Keeper and soon marriage where I will be bound by my loyalty to my wife and my children. I am bound by promises that I did not make just as I am bound to a body I did not choose. As a man, I have no control over my life it seems...not even something as simple as the woman I am to marry."

"I see," Kalima said as she inched closer to me. "But what if I am able to offer you the freedom that you seek?"

"And why would you want to do that?" I asked, surprised by my own intrigue.

"Because you and I are more alike than I realized. I want to protect you from what is to come..."

"And what exactly would you be protecting me from?"

"The Reaping..."

CHAPTER

ELEVEN

Dinayra

The vision seized my mind so rapidly, I lost my equilibrium and fell back on my bed. My body began to convulse as electrical pulses shot throughout my body. My thoughts were scrambled around in a chaotic mess, causing me to drool slightly as I plummeted further into the dimension of madness. I heard myself scream; but I couldn't be certain if it was only in my mind, or if my voice really did echo throughout the house. I saw myself spiraling into an open void of complete darkness. Time seemed to stand still as I travelled into spaces of existence that I had no idea was even real.

"Fear not," she told me. *"I will protect you... I just need for you to bear witness to what is coming..."*

Her voice acted like a cushion as my feet touched the cold hard ground. The darkness quickly gave way to a thick blanket of fog which made it even harder to see.

"Where am I?" I asked aloud.

"I have projected your spirit to the body of Neptune," she said.

73

"Neptune?" I quipped. "As in the *planet?*"

"Like earth, the celestial bodies you refer to as 'planets' are not only power sources for the Nine, but containment chambers for violators of cosmic law. Certain angels are held captive here as they are too great of a threat for incarceration on earth."

"A *jail* for angels?" I gasp. "Why am I here?"

"Follow my voice," she instructs me. *"There is something here I must show you... and worry not. No one will know you are here. Even in my weakened condition, I am still strong enough to shield you."*

"Shield me? From whom?"

"Hurry! We do not have much time. The planets are on the path towards full alignment..."

I felt a hard nudge in my spirit to start running in the direction straight ahead. The harsh icy wind blew through me, making it difficult to remain standing in one spot. The wail of the winds increased its volume, but somewhere off in the distance, I could hear the loud, forlorn moan that rocked the very ground I stood on. The temperature surrounding me dropped and the atmosphere grew darker.

"Help me," came a deep, distorted voice . "Help me..."

"Run!" Kalima's voice surrounded me.

I take off in a full sprint, no longer concerned with my inability to see what was in front of me. *There has got to be a way for me to wake up out of this,* I think to myself as I instinctively take a leap over a pile of jagged rocks. I land on my feet with feline precision and continue running blindly in the direction Kalima instructed me to do so. It feels as if I have been running for an eternity before I stop short in front of what appears to be a large tomb.

"What is this?" I ask aloud.

"It is the tomb of the old god, Titus," Kalima informed me solemnly.

"Gods die?" I ask, reaching out to touch the black stone.

"Yes and no," Kalima answered quickly. *"But in this case, he is not*

dead. He is trapped and has been since the first time I yielded my Scythe. My job is to destroy him – that has always been my purpose. To destroy those that are like him that seek to enslave humanity and take control over The Veil."

I regard the cuneiform writings with quiet curiosity as I gently trace my fingers over the carvings. An image of a dark eyed entity with massive black wings tore across my vision. I snatch my hand away and step back.

"That is Azrael, a Fallen One and the protector of Titus," Kalima said grimly. *"He is actively searching for my Scythe as we speak to free Titus and the other Nine."*

An image of Kalima, her eyes blazing in full fury as she held her ten foot Scythe in her grip. Her long locks levitating over her shoulders as she prepared to yield its power.

"I should have told Cairo the truth of what was at stake long ago," she continued remorsefully.

My heart cringed at the mention of his name, but I said nothing. It's weird: an ancient goddess of death and destruction used date my soon to be ex. If this isn't the beginning of a paranormal romance novel, I don't know what is...

"The archangels are designed to protect humanity, even though humanity is and has always been at the crossroads of self-destruction," Kalima continued. *"But there are things that even they do not know or understand... The Seraphim allowed them to lock away my spirit – they stripped me of my flesh and banished me to another realm where I was condemned to just watch and wait for the time when Titus would make another attempt to rule over the cosmos again."*

The ground shakes beneath me again and another image of the black winged angel flashes across my mind. He yields a massive black blade, and I watched as a distant bystander as his blade clashes against a strikingly beautiful angel with pale blonde hair.

"I brought you here for you to see what is at stake. Neptune is Titus' power base and also his prison. Once freed he will release the others and

enslave all forms of life- humans are not the only ones who are in danger. There are other worlds far beyond your reach..."

"But what does any of this have to do with me?" I demand, shaking my head. *"Why me?"*

Kalima paused. Her discomfort quickly became mine. *"Is it not obvious Dinayra? Look at me..."*

She replaces the scene of the two angels battling each other with her own. She stands on top of a hill, a gentle breeze blowing against her locks, her expression solemn. Her gaze locks with mine and suddenly, the shape of her eyes reminds me of my own; the depth of her cupid's arrow on her mouth looks like mine; we are of the same height and build. The glamor of her power dimmed only slightly just to reveal her true form. I suck in a deep breathe.

No. Could this...be...

"You and I are one and the same Dinayra. Flesh of my flesh. You are a descendant from one of the female worshippers of my temple – the Temple of the Black Sun. I bound her to me in the event that I should perish before I am able to destroy Titus and forever seal the Nine; the child she carried became my own, blood of my blood, soul of my soul. You are me, reincarnate."

The entire time I have conflicted with myself: my past self and my current self; my godhood versus my humanity. And just as I came to this realization, I found myself no longer standing in front of the tomb of an imprisoned god to fully conscious, laying in the center of my bed. Kalima still called out to me, urging me to find the book.

"It is within your bloodline that I entrusted the care and protection of my book," she whispered. "Your last of kin, the one that you call 'aunt' has maintained the strength of my records as her mother and her mother before her. Your father was never aware of the history of his family for no male was allowed access to my knowledge. It was my energy that protected your mother while she carried you, because even then those who reside on the other side of the Veil knew who you were. And now, time is nigh. We have to retrieve my book."

My entire life has been shaped for this very moment: to be awakened to who I once was and the power that has rested inside of me now. My aunt, the only person I have left connected to my father had always kept a healthy distance from the family. Whenever she did decide to make an appearance albeit during the holidays, she would usually just smile at me, kiss me on top of my head and focus on engaging with the adults. She wore markings and tattoos on the back of her hands that my grandmother would fuss at her for, along with the black tourmaline that hung from her neck. The gaudy clear quartz that wrapped around her finger in copper wiring always captured my attention. The last time I spoke with her was almost ten years ago...she isn't great at maintaining contact. But fortunately, she inherited my grandmother's home that was built from the ground up in the 1930's, just two hours from where I live now.

Without thinking, I push myself up and make my way to my closet. Today seemed like a great day to pay my dear old Aunt Demelza a visit; and after a quick survey of the four walls that surrounded me, there was an opportunity to get out of the house.

TWELVE

Cairo

I woke up to the incessant, noisy ring of my phone that bounced from my bed sheet and onto the floor. "Damn it," I groan, still somewhat locked in my dream and fighting to fully regain consciousness. With half of my body still holding onto the bed, I snatch the phone before the caller is sent to voicemail. "Hello?" I mumble, pushing myself up.

"Well, I'm glad you are still alive." Michael's voice said through the receiver.

"Yeah…" I groan. "What's going on?"

"On the eastern horizon, the full moon has been blood red for the last three days," Michael began solemnly. "Even the ocean is preparing for the onslaught. All of the coastal states on the eastern seaboard are under tsunami warnings. Creatures that are normally seeking shelter at the bottom of the ocean have been belching themselves up onto the beaches… and this is only the beginning… we have about twenty-four hours before she will rise."

I release a yawn and stretch every cell in my body. I'm tired of all of this. For centuries, we have all been on this wild goose chase for this one defining moment.

"She doesn't have the book. As long as she doesn't find the book-"

"She will stop at nothing to find it. The first time, she already possessed the power of the Scythe. It wouldn't surprise me that she doesn't already know where the book was hidden. Azrael tried to hide the power for himself by storing it in a book, but somehow... the book was missing."

My mind drifts back to the conversation I had with the Reapers that had protected an unconscious Dinayra... something bigger is coming. I can sense it and judging by Michael's tone, he knows it too.

"Is Dinayra still at home?" I ask just as my thoughts drifted back to her.

"That's another problem," Michael continued. "The other Watchers have been monitoring the activity levels of that cult, Order of the Black Sun. There has been an increase in their ranks and tonight, there will be an open ceremony, welcoming the return of Saturn..."

"It's not surprising," I sigh. "I've been keeping tabs on them off and on over the last hundred years. I have a feeling they have been corrupted by Azrael...I can smell the treachery of that black winged demon all over it. And thanks to him, they are almost as popular as the Church of Scientology."

"Have you spoken to Dinayra?"

Michael's question forced me to sit up. "No...I have to talk to her."

"Well," Michael began quickly. "We may have a problem. She was seen getting into her car, headed toward what is referred to as San Bernadino. They are on the freeway as we speak, but Gabriel is following her now. Do you know where she might be headed?"

My mind is spinning, racing against the wave of emotion that threatens to collide into one big bang. As far as I knew, Dinyara was the last of her bloodline. She only talked about her childhood as it related to her immediate family – her parents. As far as I knew, she was an only child, with no surviving relatives. Her mother passed away when she was twenty – two of cancer and her father followed behind her a year or so later from a self-inflicted gunshot wound to the head. She never talked about having aunts or cousins even. When I met her, she was alone. The only social support system she had was from her coworkers, most of whom she hadn't had much contact with as of late.

"Perhaps Kalima is guiding her to where the book is," I exhaled. "As far as I know she doesn't have any living family."

"I thought so. I have sent others to support Gabriel, just in case…"

"Give me about fifteen minutes. San Bernadino is-"

"I'm parked outside your house. Hurry up and get dressed. If she is doing what we think she is doing, we might be able to save Dinayra and stop Kalima before she even opens that book."

I disconnect the phone and bury my face in my hands. So, this is it. The time has come where the entire world and company of heaven will have to stand before Kalima and hope that she doesn't successfully spin her Scythe. An image of Dinayra's shy smile invaded by my sober thoughts. Her gentle spirit and soft voice that brought a blanket of comfort to my eternal soul, now turned to an ocean of grief.

"I am so sorry for what was done to you, D," I murmur aloud. "I am going to fight with everything in me to save you…this I promise."

THIRTEEN

Azrael

"The time has approached where our dark lord, Titus, Dominus of the creation realm to rise," came the voice from a hooded figure, as she approached the clothed table and sat down a large empty goblet. "Achaicus, Salomon, Castiel, Zavion, Magnus, Calypso, Tethys…Atlanta…will complete The Nine."

"I can feel Kalima's energy harnessing the very pulse of the earth," Azrael growled. "Her stench perfumes the atmosphere, reeking of dark vengeance."

"Her energy has grown stronger my lord," the hooded figure agreed. "It must mean that the book is near."

"I have every demon and every damnable spirit at my disposal searching for that book – the book wherein I harnessed her power and stored it away. We are running out of time."

"Might I suggest something?" the woman asked as she approached Azrael with caution. The Fallen Angel had folded his black wings behind his back; tucked underneath the black robing that did little to cover his hulking frame. "I did not want to speak unless there was certainty that what I might tell you is true…"

"Go on…"

"The Order of the Black Sun has existed for centuries, working underneath the cover of shadows in search of the Book of Obsidian…Our first priestess was there at the beginning of what was supposed to be the end."

"Yes. I know. I was the one who appeared to the order's founder nearly two thousand years ago," Azrael scoffed.

"Yes, and since then we have recruited hundreds of thousands of members and inserted ourselves into dozens of bloodlines… and now we shall reap the benefits of such work."

"C'mon with it. What have you to tell me?"

"One of our loyal members discovered the identity of the bloodline who serves Kalima's interests; the bloodline who took possession of the book whilst you battled the archangels; and now the only living descendant of the vessel that hosts Kalima's spirit- the first priestess…"

"You know such secret? Who is she?"

"The vessel goes by the name of Dinayra Smith…her aunt inherited the text from her grandmother who in turn inherited the book from her mother and so forth… Kalima's Chosen," she concluded proudly.

"You shall be greatly rewarded Serafina," Azrael declared, unfurling his wings. "Where does this woman reside? I shall end her life myself so that Kalima cannot return – at least not in this lifetime."

Serafina lifted her hood from her head, revealing a cleanly shaved bald head with the symbol of Saturn tattooed across her frontal lobe. "She resides in the Los Angeles area," Serafina began. "But I must warn you that she is accompanied by a Keeper."

"I believed I had killed them all," Azrael griped.

"I'm afraid not. You might remember him. His name is Asir."

"Yes, Asir...interesting..." Azrael said, his eyes turning abysmal black. "And as a Keeper he is more or less under the guidance and protection of the archangels." He lowers his gaze to meet Serafina's curious glance. "You have done well. I know what I must do... continue preparing for tonight's ceremony. Soon, the one true god of all realms, the father of the Nine will return. And Michael and his minion and all the company of heaven can go straight to hell."

CHAPTER
FOURTEEN

Dinayra

Memories that I had long buried began to resurface as I made the drive towards my aunt's house. As I merged onto the ten freeway, recollections of my summertime visits to what was once my grandmother's house that is now my aunt's house, bombarded my mind's eye. BBQ cookouts with the neighbors, the smell of seasoned grilled meat hanging in the air when the sun was at its peak; me being the only child in a household full of adults and being privy to banter that was definitely not for minor ears. My grandmother would often recruit me to assist her with the upkeep of her garden and to reward me for my services she would tip me five dollars and allow me to harvest whatever fruits and vegetables of my choice. I loved her strawberries and would pick as many as I could before my mother would scold me for being "greedy".

Aunt Demelza is my father's younger and only sister; and now my only living relative. She became my grandmother's caregiver when she had fallen ill from a stroke. Throughout my childhood, I often found myself wishing that I could come live with Aunt Demelza and Grandmother, simply because I felt that she understood me better. As a child, my parents regarded me as someone with an overactive imagination and even at one point, deluded. And when the "episodes" happened, Aunt Demelza would appear with an herbal tonic or tea, kind words and at one point, she even offered to care for me full time being that the frequent visits to a psychiatrist were weighing heavily on my parents- my mother in particular. It was like she knew that I was different; that there was something within me- *someone* within me.

"Aunty Mel," I said, fighting back tears as I crept into her room and into her bed.

"What's the matter love bug?" She asked, lifting my five year old frame onto her lap. "What happened?"

"I had a bad dream," I sniffled. "It was really, really bad."

"Oh no! Did you tell mommy?" She smoothed away a single tear that escaped my tired eyes. This had been happening for a while. Winged beasts with red glowing eyes would chase down a corridor, shrieking, "Where is she?" I had no idea who they were demanding to locate, but this was one of many recurring dreams that would haunt me the moment I had succumbed to sleep.

"She told me if I wasn't so bad, the devil wouldn't come for me in my sleep," I confessed. My mother didn't believe in nightmares. Religion told her that our sins would be the reason for such unrest and that we must forever seek redemption in order to obtain peace.

"She shouldn't tell you things like that," Aunt Demelza grumbled flatly. "The devil is not going to get you in your sleep. And you are not bad, ok?"

She gently placed her palm over my forehead and almost instantly, my terror melts away and I am overwhelmed with peace. "Soon, you will understand who you are..."

"Who am I Aunty Mel?" I sleepily asked, resting my head on her chest.

"Someone special. Now go to sleep. The bad dreams will bother you no more."

Aunt Demelza had a uniqueness of her own. Her feather necklaces, crystal jewelry pieces that she would change according to her wardrobe or mood; her henna tattoos that were a part of her daily look; the small seashells that hung from her lengthy locks that she always kept neatly twisted were a stark contrast to my father's starched and stiff business like appearance. Both siblings shared the honey brown complexion that I possess, along with high cheekbones, slanted eyes, and full lips. But that is where the similarities ended. I inherited my mother's slimmer body shape but secretly wished I could have shared my Aunt Demelza's shapely form. Even to this day as I reflect on this, I wonder how the hell was my aunt even related to my father. My father favored Christian religion whereas my aunt was freer spirited and moved by the call of her own soul instead of the texts written by man. My father held the belief that an education was the key to success in life whereas his sister was a firm believer in the school of hard knocks.

But despite their differences, there was hardly ever any division between those two – accept when it came to me.

The last time I saw Aunt Demelza was at my mother's funeral and even then, as I look back on that cloudy day, when the sky was about as dark as my mood, she said, "I have something that you will need one day. When you remember what that is, come to me."

At the time, I couldn't imagine what that would be, and I was too grief stricken to fully contemplate her ominous message. I simply nodded as she hugged me before she turned around to walk away. I remember the sound of her black pumps echoing on the sidewalk as she marched towards her car, her shoulders slumped; her long locks that were once a beautiful jet black, then almost snow white.

I didn't hear from her when my dad died almost a year later.

And I didn't reach out either. I opted to grieve alone and accept the fact that I was just destined to continue my journey through life solo. And then the migraines, the extreme vertigo and the nightmares that haunted me as a child intensified soon after, until a few years later, I met Cairo.

My heart aches at the mere thought of his name and so I grip the steering wheel a little tighter and focus on the road ahead of me. The drive to her house is silent; even Kalima who would normally take advantage of these solitary moments remained quiet. Thankfully, as I reached the exit, traffic disappeared and within fifteen minutes, I was pulling up to the very three bedroom home with the two car garage home and the sandy pathway that lined the front yard. Aunt Demelza's red Toyota sat out front, behind a black Rolls Royce. I parked in the driveway of her garage since it was the only available space.

She has been waiting for you, Kalima whispers in my mind. *She has the book! I can feel its energy and my strength is returning...*

Suddenly, a sharp boost of energy shoots through me, my body tingling from its effects. *Can't you feel it too?* She asks me, sounding every bit of ecstatic as I feel. I suck in a deep breath in attempt to ground myself as I pull my keys from the ignition. My palms continue to tingle with energy while I mentally struggle to calm my heart rate. What will happen once my hands finally touch the Book?

That sobering question nearly put a stop to my heart as I pondered the potential consequences of retrieving the very thing that I am being hunted for. Will Kalima and I merge into one being, where I will in fact be washed away as my own sovereign entity and she takes over? Will I- er, we be responsible for the end of the world? What will happen once Kalima reunites with her Scythe?

I will let no harm come to you Dinayra, she assured me. *I will only be in control for a little while. Remember what I showed you? If he rises, then the world and everything that you know will be doomed to his will. We must protect the planet from Titus.*

I then remember the quick journey to his realm and the visual impressions that his tomb left me with. His power is cold, dark, vast... even now as I step out of my car, I can sense the icy void, the chill touch of his energy. As I approach the front porch, Aunt Demelza's door swings open and she steps out, wearing a beaded black skirt and a loosely fitted blouse. Precious stones hang from around her neck while others hang from her ear lobes and wrapped around her fingers. She greets me with a knowing smile and a hard gaze.

"It's about time you woke up Dinayra," she says ushering me inside. "Come in. We do not have much time."

Aunt Demelza closed the door behind us and locked each of the seven latches that lined the door. She then rushed towards her window and closed the blinds. She then reached for a throw blanket that was tossed on the beige sectional and draped it over the blinds for added coverage. All the while, I remained standing in front of the door, just beyond the threshold, my entire being still tingling from the energy of the Book. I can literally feel the Book calling out to me, strengthening me and beckoning me to unite with its power. The sensation is both electrifying yet dizzying at the same time; I'm not sure if my feet are still planted on the ground or if I'm levitating.

"It has been too long Dinayra," my aunt began, interrupting my thoughts. "I can sense her presence within."

"You've always known...?"

Our eyes meet and her pained expression is all the answer I need. "My mother – your grandmother – may her soul rest in peace – knew as well. Your grandmother, like myself was a Seer.

She could see into the other realms, and she too was handed down the Book until it was my turn to protect it."

"Why didn't you guys tell me?!" I surprised myself with my sudden of anger burst of anger. Tears from years of feeling like I was crazy, feeling like a misunderstood outcast, not understanding that I am an actual host for a goddess of death who happens to be a version of my past self, blurred my vision.

"We were afraid to awaken you too soon," Aunt Demelza said quickly as she rushed over towards me. "There was so much you didn't know- that you couldn't know. And your father, Troy was afraid of what we knew. He refused to accept the truth about who we are and what you are. When he realized that your mother, Laura, was pregnant with you, he was afraid that you would inherit our gifts."

"So my father did know?" I ask through a torrent of tears. "He knew?"

"Troy wasn't born with gifts. The men in our family are pretty normal, with the exception of a Houngan here and there generations before us. For years, your grandmother had believed that there had just been a developmental delay of some sort when it came to his power. But it was eventually realized that he wasn't supposed to participate in the protection of the Book and its secrets. He was born 'normal'," Aunt Demelza continued making quotes with her hands, "to throw off those who would soon discover who you are- at least, that was our theory. And I think that deep down Troy resented us for it which is why she wanted nothing to do with our 'pagan' beliefs." She released a frustrated sigh. "Thanks to an extremely devout and overly concerned Christian neighbor of ours, your father became a regular guest of Mount St. Vernon which is just up the street from us and eventually a member well after he graduated from high school."

"He treated me like I was mental patient. Both of my parents did," I grumbled through grit teeth. "For years, I had to go through 'deliverance' ceremonies, doctor visits, appointments with therapists…and the pain…"

"I know. I know… I did what I could to ease you. Laura, your mother, she just didn't understand…"

"It is what it is now," I breathed, wiping away a stray tear. "At least now I understand…what felt like a nightmare now makes sense."

Without another word, she pulled me into her embrace. Her gentle sobs melted away my budding resentment, resurrecting that five year old me who loved and adored my Aunt Mel more than anything.

"I'm so sorry. Even from a distance, I felt your pain. There were so many times I wanted to tell you everything… Your 'Awakening' took longer than expected. Your spirit is strong, fighting against an entity far older and more powerful than anyone of us could imagine. But you managed to fight this long… I'm just so sorry…"

I have no idea how long we just stood there, enveloped in a bubble of raw emotion. Between the two of us, the river of tears became an ocean as every painful memory from my childhood, the isolation that I was forced to spend most of life in, my mother's detachment, the nightmares…all just bubbled over from the invisible cauldron that I carried within. As our tears began to dry up, I gently pulled away to collect my thoughts. My palms pulsed with a warm energy that grew with subtle intensity, an indicator that I am dangerously close to the Book.

She has it somewhere close, I think to myself.

She does, Kalima confirmed. *The Scythe's power is calling me.*

Aunt Demelza smiled as she wiped her face with her palms. "Our bloodline was chosen by Kalima herself to keep the Book of Obsidian, to protect it and to ensure that the vessel – which is you Dinayra – receives it."

"What's going to happen to me?" I ask, regarding my aunt

cautiously. "Is Kalima going to take over my body and I am no longer going to be me anymore?"

Aunt Demelza cringed but quickly smoothed away her discomfort. "Kalima is going to protect us all as she tried to do before. Even the angels didn't understand what was at stake."

"I know…the Old Gods are coming…"

Aunt Demelza reached for my hands and holds them in her own. "You have no idea what an honor it has been to…" Her voice trailed away as her gaze focused on the front door. "We don't have time. Come with me…"

She ushered me behind her, dragging me down the corridor and into the master bedroom that once belonged to my grandmother. I just stood there, in the center of the massive bedroom, amazed at how perfectly intact my grandmother's bedroom remained. Even her queen sized poster bed was still neatly made and not a single wrinkle. Her mahogany chest still rested in the far corner of the room…even the lavender curtains had not been changed.

My aunt locked the door behind us and rushed towards the closet, tossing out shoes and boxes until she reached the wooden floorboards. "Dinayra when I hand you the book, you need to get out of here. Do not look back," she ordered. She groaned as she kneeled down and began to rip the floorboards apart. "I wish I could stick around and guide you through it, but…" She pulled out a large black box with odd looking cuneiform type engravings etched upon it.

As soon as she lifted the box from its hidden space, my body became overwhelmed with an instant flow of energy. The sensation was strong enough to snap my head back. I wanted to laugh and cry at the same time; it hurt so bad but felt dangerously delicious. My knees buckled, suddenly my lungs forgot how to breathe while simultaneously I captured a vision of myself yielding the power of the Scythe. It was all becoming too much.

The floor beneath us began to tremble, violently shaking the low hanging light fixtures that hung from the ceiling. A loud crash at the front door temporarily captured our attention.

"You have to do this now," Aunt Demelza commanded as she sat the metal box on top of grandmother's bed. She closed her eyes and began to chant in a language that was unfamiliar to my ears, yet strangely comforting to my soul. Kalima began to shift around in my spirit, growing in strength. Her consciousness becoming one with mine. Our combined memories became a blur and soon it became a battle between her will and mine.

Let go, Dinayra, she pressed, pushing my thoughts deep into the crevices of my brain. *Let me to do what I have come to do- what we have been created to do.*

For the first time the reality of what I was going to lose, my sense of self, dawned on me. If Kalima took over where exactly would I go? Would I be forever lost in the sea that is Kalima?

Trust me. Kalima pleaded as she continued to gain strength. *I can protect us.*

I was trapped in a whirlwind of power that blocked me from assuming full control of my body. I could hear my aunt's chants increasing in volume and power. The magic of her words wrapped around me, siphoning my control.

Please! Don't leave me! Where am I going? Please don't let me die! My cries fall on deaf ears as Kalima's energy maintains a stronghold over my body. The inner me, my voice, my spirit, my soul, whatever one will call it, is instantly surrounded in blinding orb of light.

I can feel the vague impression of my arm extending and the cold hard metal of the massive Black Scythe materializing in my hand. It's power, greater than any cosmic force in the universe had been contained in the papyrus text that took the form of a thick black book. The inky words danced right off the pages as Kalima uttered the words from its binding, uniting with her power. For a moment, all I could do is watch, afraid of what the world may now become. Maybe Cairo was right in his quest to stop her. What have I done? I pictured Cairo's handsome face, his warm brown eyes and his serene spirit, now realizing that our time had indeed ran out. Now that I understand that there is a chance for rebirth, perhaps we will one day be reunited again in another life. His name becomes a whisper in my mind as the orb of light jettisoned me away from my body, from this realm and all that I had known and loved and into a void.

Perhaps I am finally free of the nightmare that felt like no return.

FIFTEEN

Kalima

It has been a millennium since I felt the warmth of the sun on my skin or the gentle breeze of the earth in my hair. Everything around me just felt so…vibrant! My chosen priestess, her long black and silver locks hung below her waistline, very much reminding me of my former self. She stepped away from the box which protected my source of power, her gaze jumping from me and my Scythe. A moment of silence passes between us before she speaks.

"Dinayra?" she asks gently.

My lungs take in a deep breath and relax. "No. It is I, Kalima."

She looked away, her expression torn between pure joy and absolute sorrow.

"Dinayra is just as much a part of me as I am her," I say. "Her spirit is safe."

Will my poor niece return? Even though Demelza's thought was for herself, it still reached my ears. It reflected in her eyes and even in her nervous posture.

Her silent question hung in the air. I can feel it in my pores and the truth is, the world is more in need of a powerful guardian than Dinayra right now. She will have her time again, to live to love and to simply exist. But as long as Titus and the Nine remain a threat, it is I who must remain in the forefront.

"Your bloodline has done well," I continue. "Had it not been for you, I would still be a prisoner behind the Veil."

"We have to leave now," Demelza whispered. "Those who hunt you have arrived. I can sense their dark energy." She took a fighting form in front of me just in time for door to explode from its hinges. Demelza made a circular motion with her palms and created an invisible shield that protected us from the flying shattered bits of wood and debris.

"Save your energy," I say, gently maneuvering Demelza behind me. "You will not be harmed today."

Loud chattering and high pitched squeals poured in from the hallway, followed by a rumbling that shook that entire foundation of the house. My thoughts travelled back to the first time I returned I from the Veil, armed with my Scythe. Both my vision and my purpose were clear: reset the balance of Time and Space so that the Nine would never be. Titus had begun his journey towards the sun to drain it of its power just as he done times before. And just as before, I came at the ready to first engage in warfare against his most powerful followers who would dare to protect his agenda. And this particular follower, I remember well.

Azrael. Once a most treasured angel, guardian and protector of magic and knowledge, fell from grace and has never looked back. His dark energy taints the air as he threatens to send more illusions.

"Azrael, you demon!" My voice bellowed. "Reveal yourself! I remember your tricks."

Instead of a reply, a concentrated ball of highly charged energy blasted from the hallway, aimed like a missile at its target towards the center of my chest. With a deft move of my Scythe, I dissolve the energy before it could burn a single fiber of my cotton shirt. I sense his presence somewhere in proximity, but not exactly in the house.

"We have to leave," Demelza repeated quickly, her palms crackling with magic. "Or else we will be surrounded."

A sonic blast just above the roof rattled the house. With a firm grip of my Scythe, I braced myself for the onslaught. Azrael could summon up demons with the flick of his wrist. An old but familiar rage became a dark current of fuel that channeled from my hand into my Scythe. The weapon ignited, its dark metal illuminating a concentrated glow of ultraviolet light. I glance back at Demelza, her long locks levitating from her shoulders, her palms crackling with her magic. From out of the ether several large black winged entities armed with similar versions of my Scythe surrounded us. My Reapers, guardians, and protectors of the dead realms; keepers of karma and assigned to follow my leadership when the time came. Even the spirit known as the Grim Reaper, the leader of the division of angelic beings was destined to answer to me.

"You are still not at full strength to do what must be done and fight in a war with both the Fallen and the Higher Beings," Demelza pleaded, interrupting my thoughts. "We can settle the score later," Demelza continued.

With a heavy sigh, I tap my Scythe several times on the floor, and almost instantly, I fold us- Demelza, myself and the few Reapers that appeared to assist me in battle- away in a blanket of energy, transporting us between the dimensions. Demelza's screams of panic could be heard all across the infinite dimensions as we traveled in between the Veil. We appear right at the highlands of former civilization that historians have tried to bury with the sands of time – Axum, Ethiopia.

"What is this?" one of my Reapers inquired. His dark gaze frowned at the abandoned gates that once protected a grand city.

"Sanctuary," I say stepping forward. "At least for now. Let's just say, the people here have been waiting for me."

SIXTEEN

Cairo

J ust hang in there D, I think to myself as I speed down the I-10
freeway, slightly surprised at the fact that there is next to
little traffic. Perhaps it was truly a work of divine
intervention – Michael – that has allowed me to quickly exit
the freeway and close in on the one location I knew for a fact
Dinayra would head to. *Please, D...* I continue with my thoughts.
Just hang on... A huge blast just a few blocks from where I am
exiting, sends a shockwave that sends a few cars ahead of me
backwards. I swerve out of the lane just in time to avoid colliding
with an SUV. The energy signature is coated with Kalima's dark
force. I can sense her anywhere. An old Honda and a blue Ford
slam right into each other just as I swerve out of the way.

"Fuck!" This cannot be happening. The low rumble from the
power vacuum seeps deep into the earth causing the street to
splinter. My head begins to spin from the chaotic backdrop of
honking cars, screams and sirens. My foot presses down hard on
the accelerator, I maneuver around the collision, barely missing a

light pole as my tire skirts off the sidewalk. *I'm too late,* I can't help but think to myself.

Within minutes, the sky darkens. From my review mirror it appears as if the sun is blanketed by a thick cloud, but upon further inspection it occurs to me that that is no cloud. It's a mass of energy created by none other than the Scythe itself. I sense the earth shifting to accommodate the power that is greater than any force in this realm and the next. And then from the corner of my eye, a series of fast moving objects jettison across the sky in the direction of Dinayra's aunt's house. For a regular spectator, these objects may look like a series of meteors that have opted to crash somewhere along the earth's surface.

But no... only a Keeper can see into the higher realms and those are the black winged Fallen followers of none other than Azrael.

"Azrael," I growl, gripping the steering wheel tighter. Azrael always held his own agenda as it related to the power of Kalima's Scythe and the Book and to my knowledge he had been cast away before he could dig his talons into the Book. When exactly had he become free?

Time seemed to stand still as I drove like a mad man for two blocks before finally arriving at Dinayra's aunt's house. Reaching into my glove compartment, I pull out my black and silver scabbard which surprisingly sheaths a retractable long blade. I've carried this weapon since my early days as a Keeper. An old god whose spirit no longer claims residence in the ethers gave it to me as a gift for my service. The blade itself was carved from lightning trapped in an obsidian alloy which allows me to kill even the highest of ranking entities – including the Fallen. Sirens echoed off in the distance, before I slammed my car door behind me, I noticed a couple of spectators emerge from their homes, frightened by the blast that rocked the neighborhood.

"Get down!" A familiar voice called out from behind me.

Instinct forced my body to move, the dark blast of energy directed at me singed the grass next to me. A gentle hand reaches for me and instantly lifts me to my feet.

"Azrael is here," Michael stated grimly as he materialized. The Archangel stood beyond the 6'5" margin when he was in his true form. His translucent wings eclipsed my view of the darkened sun; his colorless eyes offering him a grimly appearance. Attached at his side is his long blade made, while in his grip were his bow and arrow.

"She's inside accompanied by her witch," Michael grumbled. "But there is a force field that is blocking any of us from entering."

"I can feel her," I add solemnly, referring to Dinayra. "She isn't lost…"

"Perhaps we may be able to extract Kalima from Dinayra once we obtain the Scythe," Michael offered after a beat. "Have faith."

And with that he jolted himself towards the sky, where he was greeted by the hard swing of a black blade. Michael dodged out of the way just in time and double backed with a swing of his own. Metal met metal, creating a sound wave that sent everything that wasn't nailed to the ground flying backwards. The surprised screams of the human bystanders were muted by the crash and thunder of the fight taking place in the sky.

I pushed myself from the fence that I had been knocked into, ignoring my aching shoulder. *This cannot happen again,* I think to myself. The ground beneath me begins to splinter and shake, however I still manage to scramble my way to the porch. The front door had been blasted from its hinges leaving a trail of debris, broken pieces of wood and glass scattered all over the living room. The dark, magnetic pulse of the Scythe, radiated throughout the house. A sense of dread at away at whatever hope I clung to for Dinayra.

Kalima's energy hung in the airways, suffocating me with the memories from our past together when she made false promises of love and eternity. Everything always comes around full circle. I promised myself when I watched her strike down the Temple of the Old Gods with a single swing from her Scythe. Her act of defiance against the Old Ones sent a cosmic message throughout the realms. I stood beside her once, believing in her vision of a new future where there would be no suffering and that eternity would be a gift to the deserving and not only for Keepers such as myself. But soon, I would learn that there would be no future. There would be nothing more than a dark void of eternal silence for her rule over.

The villagers – my people- had welcomed Kalima into our company, with the exception of Zira. As the eve our wedding continued with its approach, my nights slowly became consumed by Kalima. Her ethereal beauty was magnetic, hypnotizing...it drew me in like the stars to the moon. Her presence alone stirred up unfamiliar emotions within me that had been undiscovered until the moment our eyes locked. But despite my growing affection for this strange goddess, it didn't stop Zira from offering cold stares in Kalima's direction or cornering me whenever she knew I was in the presence of her father.

"We are to marry in less than seven sunsets," she stated quickly just as I stepped out of my family's home. I had no idea how long she had been waiting for me to come outside.

"You could have come in you know," I said evenly.

"At this time, I no longer feel that is no longer appropriate," she sighed.

I stopped walking and turn around to meet her gaze. She had covered her face with a thin fabric, her long thick hair was piled up above her head, her demure demeanor held a hint of anger and in that moment, I could not blame her. She deserved more than what I was willing to give.

"She has lived among us for too long," Zira began. "Most of the divine beings only pass through – never settle. It is against Law-"

"I know what the Law says," I sigh.

"Then you must know how dangerous this is," Zira continued. "I have sent my petitions to the high realms. I know that I am not a Keeper, but there is no law that prohibits me from doing so."

I throw my head back and close my eyes and allow the heat of the sun's rays to calm me. A spark of irritation threatened to spill hurtful words from my lips; to deny Zira's concerns and accusations and to ultimately send her away. But I didn't . I forced myself to remain quiet and to at least hear her out.

"Kalima is spoken in a prophecy," Zira resumed. "My father discovered a text that revealed her identity. She is the goddess and gatekeeper of Time, Harvest and Destruction. She will destroy us Asir! You must listen!"

"I will hear no such thing. Harab has not mentioned such and why would he share this above all people with you? You do not wear jealousy well Zira and it definitely does not look flattering on a wife."

The low rumble of her words was as painful as the day I could do nothing more than witness Kalima destroy The Temple of the Gods.

"I will never be your wife Asir. You have shamed my family for that of a demon and damned us all. My father will be speaking with you regarding the termination of our covenant. It is for the best."

My words remained trapped in my throat as I watched her spin around and march quickly in the direction of the river where I was certain her mother and her female relatives awaited to move forward with The Bathing ritual. There by the river she would be cleansed from our promise so that she could be able to begin another offer of marriage to another suitable man in our village.

Little did I realize her words would haunt me nearly a month later as I chased after Kalima to the end of the village clearing,, despite the fact that she would reach The Temple of the Gods before faster than I could blink.

"What are you doing Kalima?" I called from behind her as my bare feet hit the wet dirt. My prized blade hung from its sheathing on my waist.

The eight foot metal conductor of energy and power levelled the monolithic structure that was the sacred space of prayer and reverence; of ancient texts; a place for the Divine. And I watched her do it.

And Zira's words haunt me now. I force my way through the house, following Kalima's energy until I reach the master bedroom where Demelza had kept Kalima's Book of Obsidian all this time. A gaping hole where the door once stood met me and allowed me entrance into the room.

They were gone. Kalima clearly teleported them to safety, which then produced my next question. Where? She could be anywhere on this god forsaken planet by now. The Archangels were high above the house engaged in a battle with one of the most dangerous of The Fallen which meant that soon not only would we have to contend with Kalima but Neptune too. Dinayra is gone and I cannot help but think that this, all of this, is my fault.

SEVENTEEN

Dinayra

I am not sure how long I've been falling. The plummet through the dark void felt like an eternity. For a while I struggled to reconnect with my body, to Kalima, but there was nothing. I couldn't hear or see what was going on. No longer can I hear Kalima's thoughts; the connection between us is lost... it's as if she discarded me like yesterday's paper when she assumed complete control over what was mine.

Why did I allow myself to trust her?

But then again, did I really have much of a choice? I know what I witnessed in those visions and those dark spaces on the dreamscape. Maybe, what she offered me was really freedom. Whatever her plans are, that is now between herself and the world. *I will let no harm come to you Dinayra,* she assured me. *I will only be in control for a little while. Remember what I showed you? If he rises then the world and everything that you know will be doomed to his will. We must protect the planet from Titus...* Her words echoed in the backdrops of my mind while I continued my plunge through the

113

dimensional realms. I knew when I crossed into a new vortex when there was a sudden shift in the atmosphere. How many worlds were there? What type of beings existed other than humans and entities that were identified as spirits, gods or better yet the supernatural?

The air around me continued to speed up as the ground beneath me became closer. Surprisingly, my collision with the ground beneath me was not the equivalent of a cement truck slamming into a cinder brick wall, but rather the cushioned embrace of a pillow. Strange. The gentle crash and roll of the ocean filtered into my consciousness. The familiarity of the sand informed me that Kalima had transported me to her world, to her prison.

So, this is my eternity.

I take a minute before pushing myself up from the sand.

"I'm so sorry Dinayra," came the all too familiar voice that seemed like it echoed from the depths of the sea.

"Cairo?" My voice is hoarse and strained from falling through the dimensions. I am almost certain that my screams could be heard in the past, present and future. I look around frantically for any sign of his presence. But all I see is the forever stretch of the water and sky. He can't find me. This time, he won't be able to save me.

"I will make this right," he continues. *"Dinayra, if you can hear me, know that I will do everything in my power to bring you back..."* As his voice begins to fade, I make a dash towards the waves, running at full speed as if I can prevent his words from being washed away by the sea.

"Wait! Don't leave me!" I hear myself call out just as my feet splashes into the water. "Cairo!"

His voice disappeared along with the tide and as I pushed myself further out to into the waves, the cold water offering a sobering embrace that I was too far away from anyone's reach – even Cairo's.

"Don't leave me..." I repeat, feeling defeated. I slosh through the water, desperately clinging on to my list bit of hope that I could capture the sound of Cairo's voice and somehow pull him towards me. A massive wave that had slowly began to build in strength finally came toppling down on me, pushing me back towards the shore. Struggling against the wave I fought to hold my breath for as long as I could, however as I tossed and turned in the current, images of old memories resurfaced among the waves.

Images of my father, his thick spectacles and even thicker mustache gave him a stout intellectual appearance. The deep baritone voice of his filtered into my mind. "Dinayra, I think your imagination is just too big for your body," he told me jokingly. "Perhaps we should cut down your TV time?" "But dad," I pressed, shaking his leg to capture his full attention. "Dinayra, I don't have time for this. I will speak to your mother about increasing the number of visits with your visits since once a week is not enough..."

Ouch. I had to be about five years old then. My parents strived so hard to mold me into a "normal" child that they ultimately pushed me away. Another hard wave belches me out of the water and onto the sandy shore. Almost instantly, my clothes are dry as if I had never set foot into the water. What's interesting is instead of pulling me further out to sea, the ocean gently returned me to land – which leads me to another sobering thought:

I'm never getting out of here. While Kalima wreaks havoc on a world that she doesn't belong in, I am trapped in a place that isn't mine. I continue to lay on the sand, weary from defeat. The only question that rests in the back of my mind is what am I going to do?

CHAPTER

EIGHTEEN

Azrael

"Azrael!" Titus' voice bellowed as the old god took a hallowed form just above his icy tomb of imprisonment. The rumble of his voice caused the ground beneath him to crack and splinter. Thunder and lightning cracked in the sky as Azrael materialized into his full form. There would be no escaping Titus's rage tonight, especially as the planets began to form the prophesied alignment. Once again, he had failed to acquire the coveted Book of Obsidian – Kalima's source of power, her Scythe.

"She carries her Scythe!" Titus fumed, directing a black lightning bolt in Azrael's direction. "That Scythe, belongs to ME!"

"There was no way for us to know where the book was hidden for eons. It was not until recently that the Book emitted power signals–"

"Silence! No more excuses!" Titus growled. "You will pay for your failure."

"There is another way to free you Lord," Azrael said quickly. "The Scythe was just one source of power. There are others."

Titus paused, while Azrael stood, paralyzed by the old god's dark glare. "Is there...? And how would you know this?"

"Like Kalima, her power was stored in a book as she was sealed away behind The Veil. When the planets align there will be an opening, a portal of sorts for you to walk through. I once collected the prayers from humanity's ancestors, wherein I travelled between the realms channeling the power from the prayers towards the reigning gods."

"What are you saying?" Titus demanded, his ghastly form becoming corporeal. He lowered himself to the icy ground, his massive frame towering over Azrael.

"There are those in the earth realm who still pray to certain deities, deities that are not as great nor as powerful as you. Those prayers and offerings can be directed to you and even to the rest of your Nine brethren. With the planets heading straight for an alignment, the power of those celestial bodies will be strengthened. Tonight, you will not require the power of the Scythe to gain freedom. You will be able to pluck the Scythe from Kalima's cold dead fingers..."

Titus' eyes narrowed as he considered Azrael's plan. "And you are certain that this could work?"

"I have no reason to believe that it won't milord," Azrael replied evenly. "May the Nine rise again."

Titus smiled. "May the Nine rise again."

"Fall back!" I heard Michael's command as he took form on Delmelza's roof . I felt the house shake as the other six archangels, Uriel, Gabriel, Raphael, Jophiel, Selaphiel, and Barachiel joined him, collectively sheathing their swords. The flames of Michael's blade were extinguished the moment his sword slid into its covering. Their robing singed from the dark energy blasts from Azrael and his demons. I stepped back out onto the front porch, defeat clawing at my insides, my mind screaming Dinayra's name. Ash and debris still fell from the darkened sky like black rain. Panic swept through the neighborhood as more sirens began to close in. In a matter of mere minutes, life as we all knew it was over. Kalima would begin her reign and maybe, perhaps, in the next life – is there is one – we might all be free of this nightmare.

"We have cleared the perimeter," Michael declared as he leaped from the rooftop and landed effortlessly on the grass. "Something or someone called that cowardice, Azrael back."

"We're too late," I blurt out. "She's gone."

"As long as she does not activate her Scythe, we still have time," Michael replied solemnly. He regarded me curiously, his colorless gaze surveying me from head to toe. "You need to get out of here. We can only keep the human authorities at bay for so long."

"I will head back to Dinayra's house to search for any clues of where she might have gone," I declare, unsure of where else to go at this point.

"All is not lost Asir," Michael said. "We will meet you there. But duly note it won't be long before Kalima will come out of hiding – and then the real battle will begin."

Michael disappeared and the urgency of the approaching sirens forced me to make a dash for my car.

"*Cairo...*" The faint whisper of Dinayra's voice calls out to me in the back of my mind. For a moment, it was like I could *feel* her running beside me. Guilt claws at my chest, even as I slide into the sleep interior of my Mercedes.

"I promise to bring you back Dinayra," I seethe through my teeth as I turn the key into the ignition. "By any means necessary, I will set you free."

CHAPTER

NINETEEN

Kalima

"Where are we going?" Demelza asked as I led us towards the direction of the dilapidated gates. Broken wire surrounded what used to be a formidable stronghold of power. As we approached, my small army of Reapers disappeared into the ethers. The factions of angels are now divided, which means that there will be chaos even in the realms of the dead.

A young woman cloaked in white robing appeared at the gate's entry. Her beautiful locks piled high above her head and secured tightly in a white wrap that added to her already regal appearance. She stood somewhere between 5'3 and 5'4", but she carried herself as if she was born to walk amongst the giants.

"It is an honor to find myself in your presence," the young woman began with a bow. "The moment my ancestors prepared for is finally here. We are ready for what is to come. Please follow me."

Demelza glances at me with uncertainty. "Are you sure this is safe?"

"Like you she wears the mark of Saturn at the base of her spine. Only those who wear that mark understand that I am Saturn in spirit, mind and flesh. Here is where I can safely gather my strength as we wait for the planets to fully align."

"Your power is far beyond great. Your enemies will not touch you here." The young woman bowed again before continuing. "My name is Marjani by the way. All ancient texts and relics of power are protected here and have been so for thousands of years. We are a stronghold of formidable magic." She paused again and motioned for us to follow her. "Come with me."

As soon as we cross the threshold of the gates, a sonic blast shook the ground and stretched further out beyond the barrier, turning the dry brittle foliage into a lush green; the shabby structures that were gates became iron strong, and freshly painted; a translucent shield rose from the ground and formed a dome over the three story edifice that survived the worst of horrors throughout the ages. The corroded bricks that lined the foundation of the structure were refortified and as we approached the rundown structure, the pathway littered with rock and debris cleared and ignited with white light.

Demelza maintained a few steps distance from Marjani and me. Her eyes remained fixed on Marjani's back, her hands crackling with dark energy. A sense of pride filled me. Demelza's soul has always been loyal to mine since her first incarnation. She stood with me the first time I stood against the heavens with my Scythe. Unfortunately, her soul does not hold the power equal to mine and she will have to incarnate again and again until she is fully awakened to her own godhood. When all of this is over, and we are standing in the center of the primordial waters of darkness and creation, the lost goddess that Demelza is, will be restored.

Marjani silently leads us between two large pillars, carved in the image of my black Scythe. A hooded figure, stood at the side of the weapon, a haunting representation of the Grim Reaper, with his hand wrapped tightly around the Scythe's base. She comes to a stop in front of a set of massively built double doors, carved from granite. The head of Sphynx greeted us as a lock with an inscription written in ancient cuneiform lined across her forehead.

"From the ashes of death her Scythe will spin, to pay the ultimate price from the debt of sin. The time will come when the Nine will rise and the company of heaven will prepare to fight. But it is Kalima, the Destroyer and the Judge of man, will save the souls of the damned," Marjani's soft voice read aloud. The doors slowly creaked open, revealing black marbled flooring. The young woman motioned for us to follow and as soon as I stepped through the doorway, I am transported back to the very first moment, I transformed my power into that of my Scythe.

TWENTY

Cairo

S irens. So many sirens began to close in on Demelza's home. As I sped off in the opposite direction towards the freeway, I could only imagine the theories that the human authorities would come up with to explain the mass explosion that shook the neighborhood like a volcanic eruption. A busted gas pipe, maybe? Or what about the sightings of Azrael and his followers? I'm sure some human thought to pull out his phone to record the battle that took place above Demelza's roof. The age of Aquarius is upon us and what humans fail to realize that the Veil between the many worlds that run parallel to this dimension is thinning. Soon it will be revealed that gods have always walked among human men and that the cosmos are far more complex and chaotic than what could ever be imagined.

"Don't leave me, Cairo!" Dinayra's voice interrupting my thoughts nearly forced me to pull over. I can still hear her. It's like I can feel her reaching for me, her outstretched hand struggling to grasp mine.

"I'm right here D," I mumble to myself. "Just hang in there." I'm not giving up hope. All is not lost. If she is still reaching out to me, then that means she is still strong enough to pull through. Kalima will not be able to maintain control of the Scythe if she is battling Dinayra.

It's not what you think, Keeper, came a distorted voice. Slowly a translucent form materialized in the front passenger seat of my car. This is the thing about being a Keeper, entities have no regard for the timing they choose to present themselves. From the corner of my eye, I notice the entity possessed the head of a dog while the rest of its body was that of a large human man. Ancient writings covered its neck and chest area, while his forearms were cuffed in gold jewelry. On its forehead was the familiar symbol of Saturn and as it regarded me, the symbol illuminated a bright neon green.

The entity spoke to me by communicating with his thoughts instead of its mouth. *A war is coming,* it said. *The realms are on the brink of divide. Protect Kalima's Scythe.*

"What do you mean, it's not what I think?"

You have failed as a Keeper, he said.

I inhaled deeply as I carefully came to a stop behind an eight wheeler. This was not the time for traffic. "I know," I mumbled. "Trust me. I know. I failed Dinayra."

It is bigger than Dinayra although, she plays an even greater part in all of this. She should consider herself lucky as the humans would say.

"Then what am I missing?" I blurt out. "For centuries, I have been tasked with the responsibility of locating the Book and stopping Kalima from obtaining her Scythe. This is the Beginning all over again... the Genesis..."

These mistakes of the past have blinded you. Even those who reside in the higher realms are fools. The purpose is to protect and guide humanity, which is noble and true. As a Keeper you are privy to things that not even the angels can see, is this not a fact?

"It is a fact." It still doesn't take away the hard truth that I failed. I failed humanity. I failed the multitude of Keepers who now rest in the realms of Ancestors. And most importantly, I failed the last person who deserved any of this...Dinayra.

Your emotions for that human woman blind you...However, she isn't entirely human. But I take it you already knew that. The entity smiled as I pressed my foot against the gas pedal and pushed forward. *She will realize that soon enough.*

"Why are you here Kemel?" I asked, feeling every bit of mental fatigue siphoning the last of my energy reserve.

So, you do know my name, Kemel smiled. *There is hope for you yet.*

"You still haven't answered my question," I said as I maneuvered onto the exit ramp.

I'm here with permission from the Grim Reaper of course, to warn you. Kalima was not created to simply reset the hands of time nor destroy worlds when the voices of justice call out for the swift Scythe of Karma. Yes, she came to the human world to escape the mundane existence of the realm that contained her. Yes, she became overwhelmed by the cruelties of man and sought to return the earth to its rightful balance. But none of that was what brought the power of her Scythe into her grip.

"If she wasn't deliberately attempting to rid the cosmos of humanity, then what could have been her purpose?"

Kemel studied me as I made a quick turn onto the busy intersection, followed by another right. My thoughts bounced between the past and the present. Images of Kalima's determined expression as she wrapped her delicate fingers around the base of her Scythe; her eyes filled with fury as she regarded Michael with the hatred of an enemy. Is it possible that we had been wrong?

You were wrong then and you are wrong now. Azrael is the protector of one of the Nine and he came to strip Kalima of her Scythe to give to Titus to make him as the supreme god. As you know, Titus is one of the Nine – the eldest to be exact. He holds power beyond what even you as a

Keeper can imagine. Kalima is the only one who can stand against him in battle. However, with Neptune's energy coming into alignment with that of Saturn and Jupiter, Titus will soon be free of his prison. And he is coming for the Scythe...along with the rest of the Nine.

"The others have been sealed away too," I said, a sense of dread coming into my awareness.

Whether you want to believe it or not, the old gods are awakening. The Great Curtain is being lifted and many of them are being restored to power. But the Nine, if they rise, earth will not be the only realm that will suffer greatly. Even the heavens will fold away and the Godhand that rests on the throne of Creation will wipe the universe and all universes in between clean. Kalima's Scythe must spin again to defeat Titus and to lock the others away. If not, there will be no hope for humanity let alone your precious Dinayra.

Kemel disappeared just as I pulled in front of the house that was nothing more than a tangible apparition of a loving foundation, I unintentionally built with Dinayra. The job was to watch her, to gain her trust and to wait for the very moment Kalima appeared to end all of this before it began – again. I was to end her life before Kalima gained too much control, but the more time I spent with her, the more she connected with me, the more I wanted nothing more than to save her life. As a Keeper, it is my job to do what must be done for the sake of protecting humanity. I am the bridge between what is of this world and what is not. Kemel was right, I had failed. The Reapers had always known Kalima's purpose -something I as a Keeper should have understood as well. But I feared what I perceived as her darkness when it really was simply her existence.

I turn the key to my ignition and the hum of my engine comes to a stop. Silence surrounds me as I continue to examine the two story townhome that Dinayra welcomed me wholeheartedly into just as she had her heart. The mistakes of the past will always return just as the rising of the sun is certain. Kalima called my name as her spirit was sealed away in a world that was supposed to be forever. I could have done something then. Dinayra called out to me when Kalima replaced her spirit with her own and shoved her into the same prison she had existed in for eons... And this time, there was nothing I could do.

TWENTY-ONE

Kalima

The magic that blossomed between me and Cairo had been nothing I've ever experienced in any lifetime that I lived. His touch alone gave me the promise of forever and sparked the desire within me to create a new world. With me no longer observing the human world from the seeing waters from behind The Veil, with Cairo, I was able to experience the human world with all five of my senses. I witnessed their pain, tasted the salt of their tears; I heard their voices cry up to the heavens and the echoes of silence that followed. Most of the lower ranking deities whose forms could be found built in the temples that the humans would pay them worship in, did nothing to aid the weaker race of beings in their mortality. I watched more humans succumb to their baser natures which added to the chaos of the newly formed physical world. Their hatred, their lust, their thirst for power over their own kind fueled the pain and the suffering that event the angels could not completely contain.

There were some nights when Cairo worked tirelessly as a Keeper to mend the fences between humans and gods, but the triumvirate of *godhood who sits just below the One, grew restless in their obedience to the orders of the One. The Nine as they are called, held dominion over the lower deities and the other, older realms that existed long even before the hands of time. And one in particular, the oldest of the Nine had watched the formation of the stars and the heavens over the course of eons. He steadily grew in discontentment over the ages; but when the sun began to rise on humanity, and the angels and spirit guides of the higher realms were instructed to protect the younger and weaker beings, Titus departed from his icy realm, and challenged the rest of the Nine to declare war on the Heavens and the earth realm.*

His call to action echoed throughout the cosmos. Demons and deities alike took advantage of the vulnerability, siding with Titus, and began demanding sacrifices in the form of blood and death. Fearful humans, desperate to hold onto their place in the land of the living conceded to their demands, sacrificing innocent children, women, animals... Cairo and the Elders spent months within the secret chambers of the Temple, performing magical incantations and spell work to seal off the holes in The Veil, from where the most dangerous and depraved deities filtered through.

But even after multiple attempts to seal what could not be unbroken.

I remember standing near the edge of a cliff, lost in my own imaginings of what humanity was supposed to be, when I overheard a group of nomads passing through the low valleys that surrounded Cairo's homeland. At first, I regarded them as I would any other group of passersby, which is until I heard the thunderous voice of Titus himself.

"I have watched you travel from the north to the south and as far as the east and west and you have still paid me, Titus, the lord and ruler of the Nine, tribute."

The humans' fear cloaked the air like a tent. I took to the airwaves for a closer view of the group of innocent travelers. This wasn't fair. Titus' presence was a threat to natural order. A god of his power was not supposed to enter into the human realms. This was an act of divine disobedience.

"You will pay tribute to me by the next moon rise or your people will suffer dearly," Titus threatened, his voice booming with each word. "For the sacrifice, I require three of your youngest, daughters – no older than twelve. Their blood must be shed by stone to prove your fealty. This is my law."

Righteous fury claimed me. This was not cosmic law. Sudden awareness of my purpose dawned on me. I am the dark energy of Saturn, the karmic reaper for injustice and imbalance. I am the incarnation of the Black Sun, the bringer of hidden Truth. Humans rest at an unfair advantage against the gods determined to enslave them. Long forgotten memories of my birthing, those first moments when I stepped out of the primordial pools of infinite darkness and wisdom, when I was called forth by the whisperings of Balance and Truth.

"The Nine have forgotten their ways and will destroy everything," I was told. "Balance must be restored. Reset the hands of Time to release the Nine from their power and all will be even."

"You will not violate those of which who do not belong to you!" I bellowed as I took form in front of the frightened humans. I raised my hand towards the sky wherein a black lightning bolt struck down in my grasp, leaving in it the power of the beautiful Black Scythe.

My gaze shifted towards the group of petrified people and my heart ached with sorrow. "You will not sacrifice any of your children. Your blood will not pay for the demands of those who seek to destroy you," I told them. "Leave. Travel as far to the ends of the earth as you can. For what will take place soon, will be the end of a beginning. Go!"

"The other gods have yet to fully awaken," Marjani began, her voice interrupting my thoughts. "But it is anticipated that it will be soon, especially now that you have awakened to your full power."

"What is going to happen when they awaken?" Demelza asked, looking around curiously. "I thought that once you awakened, the spinning of your Scythe would be the end...the final chapters humanity as we know it."

"Those who have read the stories of Obsidian, failed to understand the magic in chaos. Chaos does not always mean destruction for both are in fact one in the same," I said. "Humanity – life – is an endless cycle of birth and death. I am not here to disrupt that. Humanity will continue even through death because even death is a form of rebirth."

Demelza nodded, but the whisper of her thoughts informed me that still, she did not understand. And how could she? Her soul has incarnated several times throughout the ages, manifesting the same magical energy each time, but along the way, memories and understandings were forgotten. Perhaps when all of this is over, I will see to it that she remembers.

"Azrael has already attacked the Archangels," Marjani stated.

"As always, the heavens will be divided," I said flatly. "The love of my existence was manipulated by their ways and turned against me. He has hunted me for centuries, unknowingly to the benefit of the real enemy."

"The Heavenly factions are always in debate when it relates to humans," Marjani continued. "However, your Reapers were the only loyal entities who understood what you have been created to do."

"That is because they are privy to darker sources of information whereas the archangels reside in the light. But even the Archangels will learn the truth. Hopefully, before it is too late."

TWENTY-TWO

Dinayra

I dug my feet deep into the sand and sucked in a deep breath. The rays of the sunlike star that filtered into this realm warmed my skin and dried away my tears of frustration as I sat with my knees folded to my chest for God knows how long. There was too much that I wish I could have accomplished while I had control over my own body, other than the basics such as a degree in criminology. However, the unexplained migraine episodes, ongoing fatigue and visions of a past that I would never understand until now prevented me from living a full life. As I watched the tumble and roll of the waves gently crashing against the shoreline, I contemplated what choices did I really have in all of this?

Fate already had plans for me. From the day I was conceived it was already determined that I was the chosen host for an ancient entity that has the power to destroy worlds. Growing up, my parents forced me to attend their church, hoping to save my soul from the pathway to hellfire and brimstone. My thoughts drift back to my days at St Luke's Pentecostal, where the great Reverend Calloway stood high and mighty at the forefront of his pulpit, captivating his parishioners with his biblical interpretations of what awaits a sinner at the end of his life. I remember sermon after sermon, his hulking six foot form, his gaudy gold jewelry which hung from his neck, draped his fingers and clung to his wrists an indication of his godliness, and how his parishioners held onto his every word. By the time the collection plate had made its rounds again for the third time, it was safe to conclude that the great reverend was successful in the saving of souls each and every Sunday...

With the exception of mine.

It was the age of eight when the visions of Kalima's past memories began to blur with what was my reality. Kalima's voice became a prevalent companion in my mind, so much so that my parents believed me to be possessed – although, they weren't entirely incorrect with their assessment. On this particular Sunday I was seated in the middle of my bedroom, on the floor, surrounded by my favorite Barbie dolls, lost in the imaginary scene that was taking place amongst them. I smiled as I reached for the doll with the brown crayon colored skin and straight black hair. I named her Mona, after my best friend who was also my neighbor.

I was too occupied with Mona and her conversation with Barbie to notice that both my parents crowded the doorway to me room. "Honey," my mother's overly sweet tone held a hint of a sour bite to it. "We have someone who would like to speak with you?"

"Who is it mommy?" I asked, undisturbed by their concerned stares.

"Our pastor, the good Reverend would like to speak with you," My mother continued as she entered my room.

"He wants to hear more about your 'friend'," My father added, as he followed behind my mother.

"My friend?" I paused, after I stuffed Mona into the hot pink convertible that I begged my father to buy me.

"Your friend...the one that you say talks to you," my mother pressed. "You said she comes to you when you are sad, and she shows you the inside of her mind."

"Oh..." I shrugged, suddenly thinking about the voice that was always in my mind, telling me things about her life from the past. She told me I was special and important; and that she would always be here to protect me. "Kalima," I sighed. "You told me not to talk about her anymore..."

"Yes," my mother began as she kneeled beside me on the floor. "I know...I know. But the Reverend would like to help you."

"How?" I asked, curiously meeting her gaze.

"Well as you know, he works for God," my mother said, gently taking my hand into hers. The warmth of her hand calmed me, just like the familiar scent of her Black Orchid perfume that was her signature scent. "And he can make her go away."

The certainty in her voice gave me pause. Kalima had become such an intrinsic part of me that even then, the idea of her being separated from me, terrified me. For as long as I could remember Kalima had been my only friend. She gave me strength and courage when I had none. She comforted me when the kids at school made me feel like a freak just as much as my own parents. In her world, I was welcomed. In her world, there was peace and love. And in her world, I was perfect.

"Do not be afraid little one," Kalima whispered to me after my parents left the room. "He has no power. He is like most men you will come to know, disillusioned by his status and the lies that lay the foundation of the very building he lords over."

Still, her words were not enough to calm my anxiety. If anything, I was on the brink of panic. I sat quietly, wishing I could hide myself amongst the silence of my dolls. My parents were in the family room, their voices filled with excitement as they greeted the Reverend and his wife Cynthia. Dread claimed me and I could only wonder what kind of atrocity they would have in store for me that would worse than or equal to being dunked in a freezing cold baptismal pool surrounded by a congregation of onlookers. But the moment, the Reverend's looming *shadow poured into my room, I knew by the smile that he greeted me with that humiliation that would follow would be far worse than a baptism.*

CHAPTER

TWENTY-THREE

Cairo

Cycles, patterns, albeit life or death, chaos, and destruction, all tend to repeat themselves throughout the ages, weeding out the weak, the innocent, the guilty, until balance is somehow restored. One thing that was for certain in all systems was natural order would always find a way and little did I or even the archangels would know that Kalima was the answer to tipping the scales of Divine Order in its rightful place. Both Heaven and Hell viewed her as a threat, an abomination, a violent anomaly that needed to be exterminated. But even as I revisit those painful memories of our past, what haunts me the most in the present is the fact that I was wrong.

Utterly and completely wrong.

My role as a Keeper allowed me access to worlds beyond human comprehension. However, during those infinitely long nights when I held Kalima in my arms, I now understand how much she immersed herself in my world, while I knew nothing about hers. I knew that she was the living embodiment of the

143

celestial power known as Saturn. From the dark depths of its gaseous realm, a key to Time and Balance was created. But during the earlier periods of human civilization when the concept of Karma was considered to be revolutionary, it was unfathomable to consider the possibility that even deities – including those of higher rank – were not exempt from Karma's wrath.

Balance. It all boiled down to balance. And as I sat on Dinayra's sectional, quietly reminiscing on the mornings we spent locked in each other's arms with the sound of coffee percolating in the kitchen. I realized how special Dinayra had become to me; her laughter carried so much joy that easily wrapped around my spirit; her mind, an ever brilliant open field of intellect and thought. She enchanted me with her opinions on politics, socioeconomics, and even global warming – despite my disdain.

And I failed her.

"You didn't fail anyone," Michael's voice interrupted my thoughts as he and the other archangel Gabriel took form in front of the door. "Even as a Keeper, you too are beholden to Fate."

"Besides," Gabriel added. "Like any good story there is always a twist."

"What are you talking about?" I asked, pushing myself off the couch and rising to my full height. I regarded the both of them, as per usual immaculately dressed in black suits, resembling that of a presidential bodyguard than high ranking angels.

"Well, the Seraphim are in an uproar just as the ancestral spirits, the djinn, and spirit guides, responsible for interceding and directing prayers," Gabriel continued. "The other realms are in a bit of chaos right now."

"Prayers and energies of worship are being siphoned?" I gasp, torn between disbelief and anger. "Who is behind this?"

"We suspect it is one of the Nine," Michael stated grimly. "And if the Nine are involved, then perhaps we might have been wrong about everything."

"Azrael resistance should have been the first warning sign of their involvement," Gabriel grumbled. "But as Archangels, we are sworn to protect humanity at all costs without question. Azrael always held a certain level of disdain for humans and sought ways to destroy them. But, for all of his wayward behavior, it was never considered that he would align himself with the Nine. It is against Cosmic Law for our kind to do so..."

"He violated the Law when he turned against us eons ago during the First Divide – the Great War in Heaven, well at least the first war," Michael recalled, his gaze following the metal rail of the stairway. "Nice house," he added. "Dinayra had interesting tastes..."

"Dinayra is still alive," I grumbled.

Michael paused, his expression softening. "My apologies. She is alive."

I shifted my glance towards the painting that hung on the wall, the one of the lone sunflower that wilted underneath the sun. It was once owned by her grandmother and when she passed, it one of the few items that was given to Dinayra. Dinayra once told me that a family member had painted that and gave it to her grandmother as a gift. I remember the depth of Dinayra's reverence whenever she would gaze at that picture, and I often wondered if she resonated with the irony of the sunflower's decline underneath the light of the very sun it represented.

And now as I reflect up those moments when I catch her staring off into the painting, I realized that my sweet Dinayra may have been absolutely right.

"So, what is the plan?" I exhaled.

Michael and Gabriel shared an uneasy glance before returning their eyes to me.

"We need you to do something Cairo," Michael began cautiously.

"Which is...?"

"Talk to Kalima. Tell her that we know about the Nine and that we and the rest of the company of heaven will stand with her in the fight against them."

You have got to be fucking kidding me, I think to myself, offering the Archangels a hard glare.

"You are aware that I betrayed her once and that will never be forgotten," I said flatly. "And you two are equally responsible."

"She won't harm you," Gabriel perked.

"Yeah, but she won't trust me either. Plus, she knows that I will do anything to save D, even if that means sending her back to her own realm – again."

"We will worry about the human when we are finished with the Nine," Michael declared. "Perhaps that is her singular role – to contend with the Nine Infinite Deities…"

"But if she spins her Scythe?" I counter. "Have we forgotten the danger that the rest of the universe will face if she resets Time? All that we know will exist no more."

"That is why you must speak with her," Michael insisted. "As a Keeper, she will have no choice but to grant you audience."

I release another hard sigh as I shook my head. It seemed as if part of this hellish destiny of mine was to restore balance in my own personal life; to offset my past decisions with new choices. If the only way to ensure that humanity would be protected was to establish an amicable understanding with Kalima, then so be it. Besides, this was all my fault anyways. "Fine," I resigned. "But we still have no idea where she is. She could be anywhere in the world at this moment."

"The others have been tracking the Reapers since the incident with Azrael," Michael confessed. "As you know, she holds dominion over the company of Reapers, therefore wherever she goes they will follow. We got a bead on her in a shielded region of Ethiopia. We believe that is one of her power centers."

"I suppose I should book a flight then," I replied dryly.

146

Gabriel smiles and places a heavy hand on my shoulder. "Nope. You are going to travel in *angel* style..."

Just as I opened my mouth to protest, the two of them circled me in a shroud of bright light and the three of us disappeared, our forms deconstructing at the atomic level and transported us into the ether. I wondered if Dinayra could hear my voice screaming well beyond the other dimensions.

TWENTY-FOUR

Kalima

I took leave from Demelza and Marjani towards the rooftop of the ancient monolith that once housed Pharaohs, kings and men from a time long forgotten. This was also the same place that I spent many a night, listening to the earth cry out from the sins of humanity. At one point, I despised the curse that humans had become upon this beautiful planet. I had gone from wanting to save them to destroying them, at least until I felt the pulse of an old god.

His insidiously dark tendrils could be felt even in the seat of the universe, where I was locked away in isolation until the time came for my release. After I stepped out of the primordial pools of darkness from the epicenter of one of the largest celestial bodies in the universe, Saturn. It's power fueling my veins, some of which I channeled into the formation of the very Scythe that both the Nine and the Archangels themselves seek. From that moment, I knew the purpose of my creation. I am the manifestation of Karma, Time, Justice and Balance.

Titus, the oldest of the Nine had gone mad with boredom and an ever growing thirst for power. He held dominion in the realm similar to that of creation. There he would guard the embryos of inspiration, souls, and worlds until they are ready to evolve into the advanced stages of development. The whispers of his devious thoughts to upset the natural order of the cosmos by defying the commands of On High filtered into my underdeveloped consciousness long before I casted myself out from the protective rings of my cocoon. It was almost as if he were beckoning me, challenging me to draw my Scythe before the hands of Time commanded that I do so.

And as I reflect on the past that set the course of direction to where I am now, I realize that I acted prematurely. I was impulsive. Angry. Driven by my emotions. Overwhelmed by humanity's plight. All of this led me to my own incarceration; to Cairo's betrayal; and eons of watching from afar and waiting for the time of my return. I was even forced to watch from afar as Cairo fell in love time and time again with other women. His touch, something I will never be able to enjoy the sweetness of it again, his kiss – I could never return or savor when his lips brushed against my skin. To wrap myself in the safety of his arms, to be enveloped by the warmth of his body…

To never experience love in the flesh that was Cairo was a torment in and of itself.

As I examined the landscape of what used to be one of the greatest nations in the history of the world, I fought back tears of regret and sorrow. This time, I will do what needs to be done. And when the Nine are no more, I will return to my domain, far beyond the reach of humans, angels and deities until I am summoned forth again or until the end of Time.

Whichever comes first.

A gentle breeze surrounds me, and I close my eyes, welcoming the gentle embrace. A flash of light ignites from behind me and even with the unfamiliarity of his cologne, that scent that was nothing but pure male – Cairo – filtered into my nostrils and into my memories. I knew he would find me. He somehow always knew where to look.

I maintained my restraint when I turned around to meet their solemn expressions. The last time I stood face to face with these warriors of Heaven, I was as prepared to destroy them as well as the rest of the world. And if any of them should decide to stand in my way, I would do it again. Even as Archangels, against the Nine, their strength and power would be nothing compared to what was to come.

"What are you all doing here? If it is a battle you are seeking, I am more than ready to deliver," I began, lowering my gaze to Cairo and then the two angels, who remained silent.

"I didn't come to you to fight," Cairo said evenly. His handsome face, the same face that I once held in my hands, brought back so many countless nights of passion and intimacy into my mind. A part of me desperately desired to pull him into me, while the other half wished that he and I both never existed.

"I came here to talk," he said as he took a step forward.

"You came here to talk..." I replied coolly. "Perhaps this is a conversation that could have been held eons ago when you had a little more faith in me. Or is this more about your precious Dinayra?"

"I loved you Kalima," Cairo said, his voice filled with emotion.

"Impossible," I hissed, narrowing my gaze. "You couldn't have loved me Cairo. Not when the sun rose and set with you – that is how much I loved you. For you, I was willing to destroy and create...I would have birthed a thousand civilizations had you requested me to and yet, it was so easy for you..."

"...don't..." Cairo pleaded as he continued to approach.

"...to stick the Obsidian blade in my chest and send me back to my prison," I seethed, reliving the rage of his betrayal all over again. "My Asir...my precious Asir."

"I no longer go by that name," he told me.

"I know...I've watched you throughout the eons, hoping that I would find some form of regret...hoping to see you at least grieve over my loss...but you didn't."

"What you saw was a man doing whatever he needed to do to escape his pain," Cairo confessed once he stood less than two feet away from me. "But I did what I thought was right as a Keeper. My job is to protect humanity and to ensure that there is balance between gods and man..."

I released a slow exhale, using more strength than what I thought was necessary to gather my emotions and tuck them away in the same dark place that was once a beautiful oasis only for Cairo. "I know...that is why you and your merry band of sycophants are still standing." I paused, offering Michael and the poster child for a well behaved dog, Gabriel a hard glare. "So, you wanted to talk...talk."

Cairo smooths his palms over his face. His locks had grown out a lot longer than they had before and as he stood there collecting his thoughts, the urge to touch his face grew in intensity.

"We know about the Nine, Kalima," Cairo said after a beat. "And it will not be long before they arrive...we have come to tell you that we will stand beside you."

TWENTY-FIVE

Cairo

"And what exactly do you know of the Nine?" Kalima asked, folding her arms across her chest. Her hard glare held enough heat to melt stone. Her expression remained indifferent although the silence that followed indicated the strength of her distrust.

"Prayers, mantras, affirmations from spirit, and energies of worshipped have been intercepted and pulled away from the Source. Lesser gods are losing strength and power by the hour, while there is noticeable expansion in the hidden dimensions," Michael offered, taking a step forward.

"Not to mention Azrael's strike against us," Gabriel added.

"He was coming for me," Kalima said flatly. "He believed me to be too weak to engage him battle."

"Yet you escaped," Gabriel huffed.

"I came here to complete the binding of my power with my Scythe," Kalima confessed. "However, do not fail to recognize that I am still quite formidable, even against that of a Fallen."

"That we do not doubt, Kalima," I added, giving Gabriel a disapproving glance., to which he simply shrugged.

"Titus is an ancient enemy of mine. Our history predates that of man, perhaps resting right along the horizon of creation," Kalima began. She focused her attention on me. "I tried to warn you centuries ago, Cairo…"

"I was a young Keeper then," I explained. "The archives of Titus were sealed away even from me. At the time, Harab was the lead Keeper at the time; and he held access to knowledge and realms that I had not successfully gained entrance to through the required Trials at that time…I would not have been able to understand then…"

"If anyone is to blame for the transgression committed against you eons ago," Michael offered, his normally piercing gaze softening. "It is I. Cairo was simply the key that we needed to contain you."

Kalima paused. I watched her gaze bounce between the three of us, before settling on me. "Cairo still had a choice," her voice, shook with each syllable. "And he made his decision. Hopefully, this time around, he will choose wisely."

Guilt, regret, shame…three emotions that accompanied me through the centuries and no matter how many times I thought I had put such old wounds to rest, having buried them into my personal graveyard of poor choices and sorrow, only for them to reemerge when my heart would open its doors to another. Dinayra was the first woman that I've loved without pain, guilt, shame… it was effortless and as free floating as a cloud. Her love kept me rooted in the present; meanwhile, as Kalima continued to examine me, her dark eyes filled with resentment, her presence reminded me of our painful past.

"We will stand with you Kalima," Michael promised. "You have my word."

Kalima tore her eyes away from me and onto the two Archangels the same two Archangels whom a at one point dodged the swift metal of death that was her Scythe; whom were equally as purposeful in their resolve to stop her. And even though she was every bit of Dinayra's physical form, the power that emitted from her pores, was very much Kalima. It pained me to no unrelenting end to see Dinayra's beautiful form standing before me, but completely void of her spirit. *I know you are in there D*, I think to myself. *Just hang on.*

Judging from the silent fury that danced in the dark spaces of her gaze, I knew that she would not hesitate to raise her Scythe against us again if she felt that we would come between her and her target...or, perhaps for something much less than that.

"Fine. Titus is already preparing for his entrance into the earth realm. I can sense his movement in the cosmos...he is siphoning energy from every available source within the nine realms – including our own," she told us.

"We know. We have the other angelic divisions that are taking position in Orion's Belt, Bernard's Nebula and along the borders of each of the Twelve Houses of the Zodiac on standby," Michael added. "One way or another, he will not be allowed passage into the earth realm."

"He has already begun to disrupt the balance of things..." Kalima stated as her Scythe materialized into her grip. "Soon, there will be others that will awaken – those who are to remain hidden until the time of the Great Revelation."

"Others?" Gabriel asked in disbelief. "There is only the Nine, Titus, Oruleus and..."

"There are other beings like me that were created and brought forth only to be secreted away for reasons that not even high-ranking Archangels are not permitted to know," Kalima spat. "But I suppose, the Great Awakening is long overdue and there are those with even greater power than I whom will pick a side to join this war."

Now it was my turn to ask. "Beings such as who?"

"Ophiuchus," Kalima answered, she narrowed her gaze as she began to inspect her Scythe. "Should Titus break the barrier, Ophiuchus and his Serpent will be there to greet him – as will I."

"Kalima – "I began, suddenly finding myself unsure of what to say.

"I would advise the three of you to prepare for the onslaught. Once the Nine arrive, they will destroy everything in their wake: entire galaxies will be devoured, planets destroyed and the Veil – there will be nothing to protect humanity from the entities that are desperate to break free to wreak havoc. Once I spin my Scythe to reset the balance, Ophiuchus will heal Time and Space – all will not be lost."

"And what about your Three Sisters?" Gabriel inquired.

"They have already awakened, but they will not participate in this war. All shall be revealed in due time. Now, if you please, there is something I must do whilst time permits," Kalima turned around and began to walk towards the edge of the rooftop. "Now go."

A gentle breeze appeared out of nowhere, whipping through her hair before wrapping around her like an invisible shield. And in one quick blink, she was gone.

"As a Keeper, do you still have access to the Akashic Doorway?" Michael asked me, suddenly.

"Yes. I do. It's been centuries since the last time I accessed it," I admitted. "Why?"

"With the potential of even more powerful beings awakening, it is imperative to have a Plan B. The last thing we need are more deities roaming freely throughout the cosmos. We may not be able to destroy them fully, but if we can seal them away even for a millennium, it will give us time to figure out how to successfully put an end to all of their existence. As long as entities such as Kalima exist, humanity will always be at risk."

And so once again, there I was torn between what was right and what was *right* for humanity. I understood Michael's position, as an angel, protecting the earth realm was a part of his design. I betrayed Kalima once before and I will be damned if I betray her again.

TWENTY-SIX

Dinayra

R everend Calloway's smile disappeared the moment he stepped over the threshold of my room. His wife Cynthia followed behind him, her expression grim and I could hear my parents whispering in the kitchen. "Hello there little one," he said, offering a halfhearted grin. He took a seat on the edge of my bed, while Cynthia slid into the empty rocking chair.

"Hello," I replied shyly, pushing my Barbie's corvette towards my canopy bed.

"I like your dolls," Reverend Calloway stated. "My granddaughter has the same Barbie car."

His words made me uneasy; and I wondered why my parents left me alone with the man who terrified his congregation on a weekly basis with his reminders of Hell and brimstone. His wife offered no comfort as she sat quietly surveying my room before her deep set brown eyes, narrowed in my direction.

"What is her name?" The Reverend asked, pointing at the darker skinned doll, I sat in the passenger seat of the toy car.

"Mona," I croaked.

"Such a lovely name. I had a friend named Mona – years ago," the Reverend added, his full lips parting into a wide, toothy grin. "Do you play with any of your school friends?"

I shook my head. "No... my mom and dad don't allow the other kids to come over. They said they aren't good for me."

"Do not talk to him," Kalima's voice whispered in my mind. "He is a man who presents himself as good but he is not good. Understand?"

I made the mistake of nodding my head as if she were in front of me and unfortunately; I caught the concerned, nonblinking stares of both the Reverend and Cynthia.

"Is there someone else here with you?" Cynthia asked as she slid from the rocking chair and onto the floor. "Your mother told us about your friend. Do you want to talk about her?"

"No," I shook my head, my eyes locked to the floor. "It's nothing."

"Talking to spirits is of the devil," Cynthia's tone was laced with ice at the mention of "spirits". The tension in the room grew thick and the sense of overwhelming dread triggered the urge to dart of the room and into the closet in the hallway where my mom kept my jackets and boots.

"Let me make them go away", Kalima growled. I felt her presence shift around in my spirit. "I can make them go away."

"I don't talk to spirits," I said softly. From what I experienced, Kalima was more than a spirit. She showed me through the lenses of my mind what she could do. She was just someone who was trapped and one day, I would be the one to set her free.

"Well, your parents seem to believe that you have an imaginary friend," Cynthia insisted. "We just want to help you."

"I don't have an imaginary friend," I told them weakly. Again, Kalima's spirit threatened to overtake mine. Her righteous fury began to melt away my fear.

"Dinayra, it is also a sin to tell a lie," the Reverend said. He spoke as if my soul was already damned and as I caught the quick glance that he *shared with his wife, I could only wonder what he had in store for me next.*

Reverend Calloway, leaned forward, his large obtuse belly hung over his waistline like biscuit rolls bursting out of the can and folded his hands. He cleared his throat, still holding my gaze. "Your parents would like for you to stay with us for a little while. We can help cleanse you of this 'imaginary friend' so that you might gain entrance into the kingdom of Heaven. The Bible talks about what one must do in this particular situation in the book of Leviticus 20:27: A man also or woman that hath a familiar spirit, or that is a wizard, shall surely be put to death' – now of course, Christ offers a more welcoming solution. And as believers, we are here to help you find your way back to God..."

After that, his words were drowned out by Kalima's rage, so much so that I closed my eyes and but for a brief second, I felt Kalima's presence overtake my body. I felt myself trembling as I fought to contain her, and to contain my own overwhelming emotions.

"He will not rest one finger on you child", Kalima seethed. "This I promise you..."

"Dinayra?" Cynthia's voice cut through Kalima's promises of vengeance. "How do you feel about staying with us for a while?"

In that particular moment, I lost complete control over my own thoughts...and when I spoke, it was not my young nine year old voice, but that of someone older, stronger and of a greater threat than what even a man such as Reverend Calloway could ever imagine.

"No. It is people like you whom are a plague on the innocent; you prey on the minds and souls of the weak and the ignorant. Remove this child from the place of her family's dwelling and neither of you will know peace. Touch her," Kalima's omnipotent voice cut through the air. "And you will indeed feel the wrath of a god but not the god you deceive."

Reverend Calloway and his wife Cynthia's eyes opened as wide as their mouths. Unable to speak, I watched through the looking glass of Kalima's spirit as fear rippled over both of their smooth brown skin. There must have been an inferno which blazed from the depths of my eyes which haunted them down to the very depths of their souls because as Kalima began to retreat, returning "me" to the forefront of my psyche, Cynthia and the Reverend darted out of my room. To witness the great Reverend Calloway, stumble out of my room like a clumsy wild hog, nearly twisting his ankle as he reached the doorway, would never be enough to describe the level of horror that haunted the church leader and my parents.

I overheard him babbling on about the devil and how I was the living embodiment of my parent's sin. To them, I was a curse, a plague, a reminder of God's wrath for past inequities. Neither one of my parents spoke to me that night. I was forced to feed myself by sloppily making a bologna sandwich and a bowl of cereal since that was all I knew how to do. The next morning, I awoke to my aunt Demelza sitting at the edge of my bed, packing my belongings into several scattered suitcases.

"You will be staying with me and your grandmother for a little while," she said the moment she realized my eyes had opened. "It will be better for you my sweet, sweet niece."

Somehow, the dealings from the day prior with the Reverend and his wife made it easier for me to be resigned to my parent's decision to send me away. As a matter of fact, I wanted to leave as quickly as possible and I had hoped that the morning my mother turned her back on me, bidding me farewell without so much as a kiss goodbye or an explanation, this would be the last and final time we would see each other...

The painful memory released me from its grip and the gentle sounds of the ocean slapping against itself and the sand returned, bringing me back to my current reality. And then it dawned on me: in order to take back what was mine, I would have to fight for it. The ocean was nothing more than a sea of old wounds and traumas that I would have to contend with. The only way for me to get back to "me" was to face everything that I tried to bury. I will find my way back to myself before I allow Kalima to destroy everything that I loved...

Including Cairo...

CHAPTER

TWENTY-SEVEN

Kalima

I left Cairo and his minions on the rooftop and allow myself to plummet towards the ground; piercing the earth's crust and continuing my plunge until my feet landed gracefully inches above the scorching heat of the earth's core. Molten hot lava bubbled beneath me, the stalagmites and other mineral deposits lined the upper points of the earth's core. With my Scythe in hand, I set my focus on the power of the cosmos. I allowed Saturn to fuel me, imagining our invisible umbilical cord that bound me to the force of this celestial body, to harness its energy. It was time for the others – those who felt the sinister pull of those treacherous entities otherwise known as the Nine.

Black lightening crackles around the edge of my Scythe; wrapping around the metal in a serpentine like trail until it connected with my grip. An electric charge from the core of the earth connected with the base of my Scythe, creating a blast of ultraviolet light which shot upwards through the crust and into the universe. The surge of power from both celestial bodies

167

flooded my senses; and as I channeled the power of both sources, visions of Titus, Achaicus, Salomon, Castiel; Zavion; Magnus; Tethys; and Atlanta barreling their way across the universe, destroying suns and obliterating entire galaxies as they began to close in passed the Veil which separated earth from those ancient gods.

"Awaken!" I seethed through my teeth, my call echoing through the caverns of the earth's center. The earth began to rumble, a clear indication that I was the cause of her ire. I felt her anger ripple across her liquid core, however I continued to remain unfazed in my resolve. My Scythe trembled violently in my grip until finally, I harnessed enough energy to fulfill my purpose. I released my hold on the earth's core and materialized to above ground, in the middle of the Saharan Desert.

"It is done," I murmured to myself, offering a quick glance to the darkening sky. A flock of vultures increased in numbers, gathering in the sky like massive swarm of warning. I could only hope that the Archangels, Cairo, my Reapers and the entire companies of Heaven and Hell alike would be prepared for the incoming onslaught. Unlike the unfortunate chain of events from eons ago when Michael and his sycophants locked me away, this would be different. Innocent humans would become casualties in a war that not even their temples, mosques and churches could have prepared them for.

Not even the devil himself would be bold enough to show his face when the Nine arrived. As a matter of fact, he was hiding in a particular Garden the first time, I spun my Scythe.

"I have put out the call to awaken the others," I announced as I wandered into the main chamber which overlooked what was once part of a thriving empire, but now a modern apparition of memories.

Demelza moved away from the balustrade and began her approach towards me. The ancient markings that littered the marble floor and my symbol which marred the walls, and the ceiling held a soft glow independent from that of which the sun's rays offered as if filtered into the room. Demelza, reminded me so much of the queens of old with her fierce expression, her rich dark skin and those messy locks which hung beyond her waistline. Power coursed through her veins – the same power that she yielded in her former life when she stood beside me one evening to pledge her allegiance to me. And here, yet again, even without the memories of her former life, she maintained that same loyalty.

"I've been listening in on the news while you were away," she said. "I even sense the energies of the earth changing... listen to this..." She pulled out her cell phone from her back pocket. The hand sized device revealed images of several massive asteroids threatening to collide with earth, followed by the very concerned reporter discussing other series of events taking place in different locations around the world.

"...NASA has been reviewing images from their most recent space probe and from the looks of it, doomsday may very well within proximity of our future as mankind. Local and Federal governments are in talks as far as preparations for the collisions. According to NASA's Director, 'countries all over world should hunker down and prepare for impact from the largest of the group of asteroids, which happens to be as large as the entire state of Texas. Authorities are requesting more information from NASA with regard to the projected location of impact with the goal is hosting emergency evacuations. NASA is still working to determine when exactly the asteroids are expected to collide with earth, while both the US, China and Russia are in talks for a contingency plan to at least reduce the size of the asteroids once they have entered the earth's atmosphere."

"Tis a warning, they are a lot closer than I initially thought. The Heavenly Realms will act as a barrier to protect humanity at least from immediate extinction," I told her.

"Well, there is more," Demelza continued. In a deft move, she clicked on the next video and held the phone to my face. *"Environmentalists are struggling to answer a mind-boggling question that seems to have top experts stumped: A vast gathering of vultures are acting as sentinels over an opened crater that geologists are struggling to explain here in the Sahara Desert. An earthquake measured at 7.9 rattled the sands of the most famous desert with the aftershock still being felt for miles..."*

Demelza ended the video and played another, her expression solemn. "..If you thought global warming was a problem," the reporter began after clearing her throat. "Then you might want to consider this: over the last few days, underneath the surface of the Japanese archipelago, otherwise known as Japan, the underwater volcano, known as Fukutoku-Okanoba has begun showing signs of activity which has the national government concerned..."

"And this is not the first one," Demelza added, turning the volume of her phone down. "It is happening all over the world."

"Even the earth herself is preparing for the destruction that is to come," I said grimly.

"I can use my magic to slow some of it down," Demelza offered. "But the act itself will consume vast amounts of energy –

"Do not trouble yourself with such matters. Natural disasters as humans prefer to refer to the earth's reaction to their mere existence, has always and will always remain a threat towards humanity's survival. Plagues, floods, famine, earthquakes, tsunamis... those are things that we are not purposed to stop. We are here to destroy the Nine to restore the balance of not only earth but for every realm. When the time comes, we will bind Azrael and cast him into oblivion for his crimes. Reserve your energy. You will need it."

Demelza nodded and turned away as Marjani appeared from the corner of my eye with her approach.

"The Order of the Black Sun have sent out their emissaries as a distraction," she said quickly. "They've arrived a few miles west and are in route in an attempt to take your power."

I close my eyes and inhale deeply. "Worry not Marjani. I am at full strength. They cannot take what is not theirs to own."

Demelza's hands crackled with concentrated purple light; her dark eyes ignited with the same energy. Her righteous fury fueled her magic and a sword with an obsidian handle and a violet flame as the blade materialize in her hand.

"Allow me to offer them a proper greeting," Demelza smiled wickedly.

"Be my guest," I said, returning the grin. "Far be it from me to deny the Order of the Black Sun a proper introduction."

TWENTY-EIGHT

Cairo

"Twenty Nine people died in a mass suicide in nine underground churches known as The Order of the Black Sun," the news anchor began solemnly. "According to local author authorities, the body count totals to two hundred and - one victims, ranging in age from twenty one to seventy – seven. Reports say that the acts were the result of an occult ritual and that all of the victims used nine inch daggers with obsidian handles which was used to customarily cut their wrists which is what appears to be the main causes of their death…"

"Ah, the cursed Order of the Black Sun," Gabriel grumbled, taking another hard swallow of bourbon.

"They are doing the blood sacrifices again," Michael added. "How long has it been since they performed this kind of savagery?"

"Centuries," Michael replied, setting his now empty shot glass down. He glanced around in search of the waitress, who had disappeared in the kitchen to assist with another order. "It's so hard to find good service nowadays."

"I see that the valiant and noble Michael woke up on the wrong side of the bed this morning," Gabriel snickered.

"With humanity being in the current state that it's in, you know somehow always on the brink of a natural disaster, or famine, or a pandemic... not to mention the technological advances that could not only wipe out an entire country but the world. Then there are the matters surrounding the overall corrupt natures of human souls that lead to things such as murder, rape, crimes against children –

"We get it," Gabriel interrupted. "Humanity has been on a downward spiral towards self-destruction for a very long time. No need to stress yourself out about now champ. Once all of this is over, we will have millennia after millennia to worry about saving humans from themselves. Right now, we need to focus on the fact that very old but powerful gods are traveling through the dimensions to wage war on humanity."

"They don't want to wage war with humans," I murmured, capturing the attention of both archangels. "As a Keeper, I was privy to information to things that even you Archangels weren't."

I paused to reflect on the direction of my thoughts. I was a newly initiated Keeper at the time Kalima first introduced herself to our plane. However, I still accessed the Akashic Hall of Records – which was the main realm of record where I learned everything I needed to know about every god, every spirit, every angel, devil, demon, creatures that are now main characters of myth and legend, and every blessed or charmed weapon that was ever in existence.

With the exception of Kalima.

However, the realization of Kalima's purpose and the reason for the high heavens managing to maintain the greatest secret every kept, brought forth a surge of memories of what I learned when I wondered the halls of the Akashic Realms.

"The Nine seek power – infinite power," I continued, toying

174

with my empty glass. "It is no surprise they've intercepted the airways to channel the spiritual mediations, supplications, chants, and devotions. The lesser deities will soon weaken; and the humans connected to those deities will suffer unknown consequences as a result. The Veil will collapse on itself."

"It will take nearly every warrior angel at Heaven's disposal…"

I interrupt Michael with a hard sigh. "Unfortunately, Kalima is the only one with the power to destroy them."

"And what about Ophiuchus?" Gabriel demanded. "The Serpent Holder is not to awaken until he is called."

"Kalima will call him," I answered. "My guess is she is his destined counterpart. It all makes sense now. I didn't have access to the higher realms of the Akashic Halls; however records of Ophiuchus were always accessible to even the newly initiated Keeper. His books mentioned his awakening, but it was expressed that it would be his equal that would summon him."

"And what are to do with him when all of this is done?" Gabriel demanded.

"His constellation is really a doorway to his own realm," I told him. "He has no place outside of it. He is in possession of too much power. His awakening may further disrupt the balance. The only saving grace about Ophiuchus is he will balance out the power of Kalima's Scythe."

"We can only hope that it will," Michael sighed.

"How long do you think we have before they arrive?" Gabriel asked grimly.

I released another hard exhale and blankly stared at the flashing digits on my phone. "Twenty- Four hours, tops."

TWENTY-NINE

Azrael

Azrael stepped back as Titus rose to his gargantuan height, his sharp silver eyes glared down at the now terrified Azrael, he clenched his fist, admiring the black flame that emitted from its grip. "Yes," Titus growled with pleasure.

"I am free...it has been eons...EONS, since I've traipsed across a sea of stars or observed more than just the passing of time. Ensuring the survival of newly formed souls – seeds of potential power up for grabs – to pass through to fulfil whatever fate assigned to it, was once a great joy of mine." He glanced down at the entity known as a Fallen, his cheeks parting to expose a toothy grin. Dark power oozed from his pores and with trembling hands, he peered into the icy realm that imprisoned him.

"Do you know what it feels like to be stripped of your divinity and forced to a fate of isolation? So close to death but not close enough to walk through its doors?" Titus queried, returning his focused gaze to Azrael.

"I could only imagine...I nearly shared a similar fate a millennia ago," Azrael replied. "Had it not been for you my liege, I might've been trapped in the Euphrates River like the rest of the heavenly idiots."

"Prayer is a powerful source of energy," Titus began. "Laced with love, belief, hope, - humanity's trinity – it is the divine umbilical cord which connects humans to gods."

"The others have awakened and are making their way here," Azrael announced. "I could hear the war cry of Zavion from all the way across Orion's belt."

"Speaking of Orion, I felt his presence growing in strength," Titus said coolly. "Has he awakened?"

Azrael's black wings spread open, and he pushed himself off the ground, taking flight to meet Titus's face to face. The old deity, who reminded him more of an archon or a titan than a god waited for him to speak.

"He has risen. Kalima's call to action caused a cosmic rumbling…the entire company of Heaven in rings one through four have emptied out in preparation for battle. Hell has even begun consolidating its forces, which for me is a bit of a surprise."

"Let them come," Titus growled as he took one step forward. "Have your warriors clear a path. Decimate as many Archangels as possible- especially that painful irritation known as Michael… exterminate all guardian spirits, and all other entities who dare to stand in our way. They took what was mine eons ago and I am here to reclaim it."

"As you wish," Azrael said with a slight nod. "We are too close to victory. I will not fail you!"

Titus raised his massive finger and offered Azrael a hard nudge into the atmosphere. Azrael's black wings propelled him upward and out of Neptune's gaseous clutches. Vengeance was always a dish best served cold and finally, Michael and the complete company of Heaven finally would pay. One way or another, the entire universe and all of creation would bow before a greater god;

and once Kalima's power was returned to the pages of the book, even Titus and the rest of the Nine would lower their heads before him.

Dinayra

God only knows how long I spent walking along the endless coastline. It just seemed like both the land and sky stretched on forever, with no other possibilities of change. Even when I trudged up the sloping sandy hillside, I found myself facing nothing but open water.

"This couldn't be all that there is to this prison," I grumble to myself. Any hope for an inland became nonexistent. "She couldn't have spent the last few thousand years confined to just this..."

I stopped to survey what was in front of me. The rush of the waves beating against the shore drowned out most of the mounting panic that was building a fortress in my mind.

"She's a goddamn goddess," I muttered under my breath. "With her power she could have completely redecorated this place with a wave of her pinky..."

A flash of an image took over my mind's eye, a split second visual of Cairo, standing in front of her, his expression masked by that of pain and regret. Two immaculately dressed men flanked him; their colorless eyes adding to their already otherworldly appearance. I stopped walking and tried to refocus my mind's eye, to reconnect with Cairo in some way just to let him know that I am ok... I am still here.

"Cairo..." I whisper just a gentle breeze wraps itself around me, leaving me with the subtle impression that the utterance of his name will be carried off into the wind and delivered to him. I released a slow exhale and released the buildup of tension to allow myself to focus.

"Just breathe," I murmured to myself. "I can do this..."

After several deep breaths, I found myself taking a dive into the deeper spaces of my mind. Pushing past the void of darkness, and suddenly, my psyche is flooded with images of my form materializing onto the rooftop of a stone monolith. Through her eyes, I can see the far reaches of land that extend well beyond the horizon. Wherever she is, from what I could gather, this felt like her power base. I could see the outline of the main city miles away from where Kalima stood.

She spun around to meet the cautious gaze of Cairo. His locks bristled in the wind, his expression appeared worn, as if the weight of the world had grown too burdensome to carry. She was aware of my presence and allowed me room to bear witness to their conversation. Her pain wrapped around me, coating me with her despair. Her anguish filled my lungs as she fought against the urge to pull Cairo into an embrace. Her resolve, however remained strong and as I sat back and listened to the conversation between two former lovers and the pending threat against humanity.

I will release you when all is done, Kalima whispered to me. *But if I do not stop the Nine from coming, there will be nothing left for you to return to.*

She jettisoned me back to her prison world of endless sky and sand and when I opened my eyes, free of the connection. My heart ached to return to the mundane existence that was my life. A part of me wanted to believe that Kalima would honor her word by releasing me once she had accomplished her purpose. However, the old flame of love that she carried with her throughout the ages grew in strength at the mere sight of Cairo triggered the flame of righteous indignation within me. This was *my* life she had completely taken over. A sense of dread claimed me as surveyed the infinite overlapping of waves that made the sea. In order to fully gain control over my body, I have to swim through the darkest depths of my personal psyche. Kalima trapped me within myself, in a space so deep, and so far out of my physical reach that I had no idea it even existed. And because we are somehow connected, this world mirrors that of what she experienced for centuries.

I slowly began my approach towards the water, becoming more determined with each step. "I can do this," I remind myself as the waves gently brush up against my feet. "These are nothing but moments of the past- and if I can deal with the past, then I have control over my future." I continue walking until I am completely submerged underneath the murky depths. Most of my life was spent being overrun by Kalima's presence. There was no way I was going to just give up now without a fight.

There has to be a way to separate her spirit from mine, I think to myself as I continued to drift into the watery abyss. *Well, there is only one way to find out....*

CHAPTER

THIRTY

Kalima

D
emelza was the first to exit the tower to greet the incoming flashes of dark magic. Her hands ignited with a white hot energy and after extending her arm to the sky, she slammed her fist down to the ground releasing a sonic wave which redirected the flares of dark magic back to its appropriate senders. I followed behind her, taking a heroic leap from the balcony, armed with my Scythe. I allowed myself to free fall to the ground, embracing the velocity from several stories above the ground. The earth welcomed me as I landed with the grace of a feline, in just enough time to deflect a black charge from incinerating Demelza where she stood.

A hundred witches from The Order of the Black Sun surrounded us. All of them willing to meet the promise of death by my Scythe. I felt their insidious energies increasing by the century while I was trapped in my prison. They submitted to Azrael's rule in hopes of the promise of an extended mortal life and power, using their natural gift of magic for his gain. I knew the day would come when I would have to confront them. Most of the women who stood before me with hardened resolve that permeated through their dark gazes, were descendants of the first shamanic peoples who appeared shortly after the first war in heaven. It was shameful to bear witness the perversion of such abilities, of such talents that were meant to aid humanity toward its collective ascension. But alas, here we stand...

"I would like to warn the lot of you," I began, clutching my Scythe tightly in my grip. "I do not wish to war with you. As a matter of fact, I would rather much inform you that you are on the wrong side of a battle that will not be won by the entity you worship."

"I beg to differ," came the approach of whom I assumed to be the leader of this small army of dark magic. She yanked the black hood from her head, exposing a head full of straight raven black hair. "That Scythe will be returned to Azrael, Kalima as you will returned to whatever dark realm you belong."

"Serafina," I growled, my eyes blackening with rage. "You and your sisters have been misled. I am Karma incarnate; the ultimate Reaper – even death itself retreats from my presence..." With all my strength, I slam the Scythe to the hilt into the earth. A black lightning bolt strikes across the sky, its energy siphoned into the Scythe and absorbed into my grip.

Serafina and her army of dark practitioners begin to chant, using the spells from a past that no longer exists in recorded history. Their words filled the air, drawing in darkness to surround the territory. An insidious sense of foreboding cloaked the atmosphere as they began to concentrate their power. Demelza's voice rose above the others as she opened a channel which connected to the other side of the Veil. Several large entities stepped through, their transparent forms blending with the surrounding darkness, as they circled the gathering of witches. The chanting ceased and through the lenses of my peripheral vision, the largest of the entities raised a tightly clutched fist high into the clouds before slamming it directly over Serafina. The witch glanced around in confusion as she realized that she had been confined to the invisible boundaries of his hand. The other entities followed suite, imprisoning at least half of The Order's minions.

I release the current of energy that flowed within me from the Scythe, weaving my rage into its fabric of energy onto Serafina and her followers. Their screams carried into the heavens as they were slowly consumed by the blast; their physical forms melting away to ash.

"Kalima!" A voice ripped through the atmosphere, instantly capturing my attention. I looked up to the sky to notice the black wings of an old assailant, an enemy as old as Time itself. Azrael.

I yanked my Scythe from the ground as Demelza took position beside me. Her skin crackled with magic; her eyes lit with fire. The tension in the air thickened as we waited for his approach. He took his time with his descension. I regarded him the way a lion would an approaching opponent, my eyes never leaving his gaze, muscles tense and ready for the slightest offending movement. The moment he landed, his semi naked form transformed to reveal a black business suit, his black wings no longer visible.

"Impressive," he said as he approached. "I almost forgot how theatrical you can be."

Without a word, I issued a black volt – a warning – in Azrael's direction. He barely dodges the strike by a hair; and he coolly dismisses the singe mark left on his blazer.

"I need a moment of cease fire my dear," Azrael began, raising both hands up in a mock surrender. "I come in peace."

"Since when does a demon of your ilk concern yourself with peace?" I demand as he took another step forward.

"I know that you are here to destroy the Nine, Kalima," He

began carefully. He stopped just an arm's length in front of me, the tip of my Scythe pressed against his chest. "We share mutual goals."

"You are the cause of my imprisonment," I hissed. "I could have ended this a long time ago"

"I now see the error of my ways," Azrael groaned, his expression filled with emotion.

"Do not trust him," Demelza seethed from behind me.

"If Titus is successful in ending your pathetic life and acquiring the power of the Scythe, all that we know will cease to exist. Hell will belch itself into oblivion; heaven will collapse; and humanity will be enslaved to the will of a dreadful god."

"You don't care about humanity," I scoffed. "You are a Fallen, an entity who opposed both the creation and the angelic servitude towards humankind."

"Ah but I do…" Azrael's lips parted to expose a set of perfectly white teeth.

"What do you want?" I demanded.

"Asir- Cairo – whatever he calls himself these days," Azrael continued. "The love of your existence, the one who betrayed you eons ago…"

I frowned and pushed the Scythe deeper into his chest. He recoiled and took a step back, his colorless eyes examining my face. "For a goddess of destruction, you are indeed quite beautiful. It is shameful to think that someone of your power would find herself a victim of betrayal by a Keeper no less."

"That was a long time ago," I hissed. "Tell me what it is that you want or simply die here."

"I know that deep down in that beating heart of yours Kalima, that you still care for the Keeper – he is the last one after all. I would be more than happy to ensure his survival…the life of a Keeper in exchange for the Scythe."

"Killing him would guarantee your demise," I say calmly.

Azrael's grin widened. "Indeed. But let us not forget the

importance of Keepers. They were created to prevent entities such as you and I from coming to blows and inevitably destroying humanity. As a matter of fact, they have access to all records of life and all measures of existence. They are Guardians of the Akashic Halls."

"To kill a Keeper – and one that is as heavily protected as Cairo – will ensure a fate within the Abaddon Pitts – which is where I am about to send you…"

Azrael disappeared into the ether, leaving behind empty foot sprints from where he stood. "As you wish Kalima," his voice echoed in the wind. "Cairo's blood shall be on your hands much like the rest of the Keepers who dared to stand in my way…."

"I should have taken his head," I vehemently spat. Fury cracked open ancient wounds from memories that travelled beyond the past. "He was right here and I should have lopped that interlopers head from his shoulders!"

"You will," Demelza said calmly, her gaze serene and fixed on the sky. "Look, Kalima…" She pointed in the direction of two orbs of bright light: one neon green and the other a bright blue, travelling at a speed faster than that of a meteor through the earth's atmosphere. "They are here.….Ophiuchus and Orion… they are here."

"Then it is time," I said with a heavy sigh. "Prepare to open the Veil for the others to pass through. I hope the Archangels are prepared for the onslaught." I pause, reflecting on my tense conversation with Azrael, suddenly curious as to why he would take such a risk to negotiate with me. "Azrael's betrayal is what we can possibly use as leverage or even as a divisive tool for Titus and his brethren to bicker over… they might even save me the energy and destroy Azrael himself."

Demelza nodded as she took one last look at the sky before walking in the direction of the tower where Marjani waited. The ashes of the fallen witches, servants of The Order of the Black Sun, was swept away with the wind. Their pain filled screams of terror now a memory as their souls no longer bound to the mistakes of this world, they are now baptized in death. Perhaps in the next lifetime, their wrongs will be balanced out with better decisions. But as for me, this will be my last incarnation on this plane for it was never written for me to exist beyond the death of the Nine gods. I will return to the protection of Saturn's womb and remain there until called forth again. Peace is all that I yearn for in the next millennia. The stillness of the void, the silence of the darkness enveloped around me, along with the pulse of the celestial body offering its rhythmic tune as a lullaby. Cairo, along with the rest of the world will be able to exist well into their purposes – that is until, the next cosmic event. Maybe, there will be a space for me to exist as I am, in a world of love and laughter, pure hearts and overwhelming joy in another time or even dimension.

And maybe, just maybe, Cairo and I will be reunited there.

CHAPTER

THIRTY-ONE

Cairo

I left Gabriel and Michael at the lounge and took leave to my loft, where I spent the last three hours searching through my belongings for a particular weapon, Harab handed to me the night of my initiation as a Keeper. As I plowed through the depths of my walk in closets that were nearly as large as a bedroom, I thought about the earlier days of civilization. Experiencing the rise and fall of the sun during the period of humanity's infancy, are memories that I will carry with me for the remainder of my existence. My tribe, the original Spirit walkers, Keepers of text, Scribes of History and Guardians of the Akashic Records, were bound to mediate between the physical realm and the worlds that exist beyond the Veil. Only the select few were gifted with immortality to ensure the survival of the role of the Keeper.

And I am the last of the Keepers.

The eve of Kalima's imprisonment, as I tracked her to the furthest corner of the world with the aid of the Archangels, my entire clan was decimated. From the eldest of the Immortals to the youngest of mortals. When I returned home to seek healing and refuge within the arms of my people, their blood called out to me from the soil and the silence that blanketed a once thriving and vibrant community of people was near maddening. It siphoned what was left of my grief and transformed the depths of my despair into rage. The rumor that pierced the airwaves suggested that it was Kalima who slaughtered them. However, I knew Kalima loved my people just as much as she loved me. The children flocked to her like bees to a flower. She held them, kissed them, and allowed them to teach her songs. It didn't take long for the Elders to gravitate towards her. They asked her questions about life after death and the worlds that existed beyond what they were allowed to see. She reassured them that life beyond the flesh was more exciting than what they were experiencing in the land of the living. She taught them secrets about her world and even strengthened their own psychic abilities wherein they were able to "see", and dream walk amongst entities that only a trained Keeper could communicate with.

Kalima might have been many things, but to spill the blood of the innocent, which was not within the boundaries of her character. There are hundreds of different deities who could have capitalized on the chaos of Kalima's presence, however, one entity comes to mind when it comes to spilling the blood of humans. Azrael. That treacherously duplicitous bastard relished the idea of human destruction: that was after all the reason for the First War and how he came to be cast out of the heavens.

A grounded angel, one with wings but cannot seek refuge in the heavens, was a dangerous one. Unfortunately, he was one of the few who managed to escape punishment and it was no real mystery to uncover when it came to identifying Titus' loyal follower. Harab and the other Keepers had warned us to be wary of any one of the Fallen.

"They will seduce you with profound knowledge," he said. *"Tempt you*

with all of the powers of the earth. But they are no redeemers of souls; only devourers of all that is human. They wish to rule as gods but have no kingdoms. Be careful, always..."

And as the image of Harab's stark features came to mind, I found the small gold box that I had tucked away from the eyes of even the Archangels: the Babylon Blade. It was bestowed upon the first Keeper by Anubis, one of the Guardians of the dead as a gift from Osiris. It was handcrafted by the Babylonian god of fire, Ishum, meant to slay the Fallen. The sharp end of the blade was molded from the spark of a captured lightning bolt. Cursed with the flames of the underworld, which is overseen by Osiris, this is the Keeper's ultimate weapon. With so many entities that respected and admired our roles, there were an equal amount of those who didn't – namely angels who disobeyed Divine Order. It was the last resort to ensure the survival of the Keepers and never to be used indiscriminately.

"I see you have held onto that weapon," a velvety voice pierced through the silence, interrupting my thoughts. I jumped up quickly, bumping my head on the nearby rack of Tom Ford clothes I used to protect some of my secret artifacts from prying eyes.

"What do you want reaper?" I sighed, suddenly feeling annoyed. "I don't have time for any more riddles."

"It is not riddles you should concern yourself with Keeper," He said evenly. "Harab taught you well."

"What is it that you want?" I said sharply, standing in the center of my closet, suddenly feeling trapped by the mountains of clothes and stacked shoes, artifacts and other odds and ends that would give the most prominent collector a hard on.

"The Babylon Blade is not only a weapon but a key," he continued. "I thought as a Keeper you would know that."

"My mentor was killed before I could fully complete my training," I said flatly. "I knew the power that this dagger possessed and what it meant as a means of protection." I paused and looked down at the gold box. "Tell me more about this 'key'."

"If you are considering using that on who I think you are, that is perfectly fine with me. Azrael has always been quite problematic, but I digress. When all of this is over, Kalima will have to return to her power source. She will be needed again in the future, and we cannot risk her demise if she resides here in the earth realm too long."

"What are you saying?" I ask.

"When all is done, when the Nine have been completed, you are to pierce that blade into Kalima's heart. Not only will it send Kalima back to her gestational realm, but it will bring your beloved Dinayra back."

"But won't it kill Dinayra in the process?" My voice trembled at the thought. "There has to be another way."

"Dinayra's fate is in the hands of On High now. The Plan has always been greater than her."

"Yeah but, you are asking me to betray Kalima again and potentially kill my beloved."

"This is the only way," the reaper's voice carried a hint of sorrow. "You are a Keeper. What must be done will be done."

THIRTY-TWO

Azrael

"You will pay for your treachery!" The voice of an ancestral spirit from an ancient past echoed throughout the cosmos. His transparent form became corporeal as he stepped out of the folds of blackness, armed with a long blade, lined with the markings of his people. Behind him more than a thousand of his deceased bloodlines appeared behind him. Each of them held the same righteous rage as their leader.

Azrael remained unmoved by the spirit's declaration. The backdrop of stars that extended beyond his line of sight would bear witness to the pending bloodshed that would forever stain the cosmos. More spirits appeared, ranging in age, rank, and bloodline, forming a protective line as a means to prevent Azrael, his followers and the Nine from breaching Orion's Belt. The cluster of stars mixed with gas that circled around the gateway of Orion, thickened, as if on instinct.

"You will stand aside lest you find yourselves meeting a second death," Azrael seethed.

The loud blast of a trumpet echoed throughout the galaxy. A streak of bright light sliced through the darkness and a multitude of heavenly bodies appeared from the envelope, taking position in front of the seemingly endless group of spirit guides. Warrior angels held their resolve as Titus propelled himself to the front of the Fallen, his massive form hunkering over most of the entities that stood prepared for battle.

"I am older than your recollection of your first beginning, and older than your understanding of Time itself," Titus began, the power of his voice alone caused a nearby star to collapse on itself "I transcend the rules of creation, life and death and you all dare to challenge me?"

"You will not break this line," came one of the angels Azrael knew to be Malak. "Turn away and return to your assigned stations Titus," Malak continued, gaze darkening as he regarded Azrael. "A war with the company of Heaven is not what you wish."

"What I wish," Titus began, his black eyes shifting to a midnight indigo hue. "Is for the lot of you to get out of my way."

Before Malak could brace himself, Titus yanked the angel from his position, crushing him in his grip. As Malak struggled to break free, one of his magnificent white wings snapped off. In a deft move with his free hand, plucked Malak's head from his body and casually casted the remains into the weightlessness of the solar system. The warrior spirits, guides and angels looked on; their expressions frozen in horror. It seemed as if Time had finally stood still, the only sounds to be heard were the low buzz of frequency emissions from the nearby celestial bodies that continued with their journeys around the sun.

"Now," Titus continued, returning his dark gaze onto the collection of warrior angels and spirit guides. "What will it be?"

The ancestral spirits released a collective war cry, a call to battle which rattled the heavens, shook the stars, and echoed into the depths of the distant planets.

"We will not rest until the Nine are defeated! To victory!"

"In the name of the On High! We fight!"

Foolish sycophants, Azrael silently brooded as he brandished his black blade. From his peripheral vision he noticed the other eight gods take position beside him. Calypso, Guardian and Keeper of Prophesies curiously regarded him. Her long strands of silver hair reached out to him like the tentacles of a squid. Those radiantly piercing snow white irises burned a fiery red, matching the flames of her fury. Comparatively, she was the smallest in size next to her kin, but still significantly larger than Azrael by several meters.

Azrael felt the burn of her stare and found himself slightly annoyed. "Notice anything different about me?" He asked snidely.

"Why yes," she answered quickly, her voice sounded like a thousand ringing bells. "As you know I am the key to the future. And your future...holds nothing but blackness. Be mindful of who you betray."

Her words clung to him like a heavy cloak while simultaneously exposing him to his own truth. She turned away from him to face the approaching squadron of warrior angels. Azrael stood back and looked on as another war of the heavens took place right in front of him. He was too close to victory to be distracted now. The hard chime of a blade in his direction returned his focus and he dodged the swing just in time.

"Betrayer!" yelled the ancestral spirit as he launched another attack on Azrael. "You dare to follow this wretched being to your own death?"

"Death is guaranteed when you protect the weak," Azrael growled between clenched teeth. "And you. Are. Weak." Azrael doubled backed and with a hard lunge, the tip of his blade successfully pierced the center of the spirit's chest. Azrael hung back as the being disintegrated into white light.

"Michael should have locked you away with the rest if your ilk," came another warrior angel, his wings ignited with the flames of justice.

"Is that so?" Azrael grinned. "Then why don't you finish what Michael started?"

"Don't mind if I do..."

CHAPTER

THIRTY-THREE

Dinayra

There is something about drowning that is perhaps the most terrifying way to die. One's consciousness is fully aware of the present reality; the heart is working in overdrive to function as it is programmed to, but like an overworked machine, it will eventually begin to implode, shutting down its function, until it no longer ticks. The lungs silently scream for an inhale while the rest of the body is begging not to; and should one give into the lung's demands, the body is no longer a suitable host for life; and instead becomes a vessel for death.

But deeper into the depths of my psyche I sank, unable to breathe as memory after memory bombarded my vision. My past pain weighed me down like an anchor, pulling me away from the surface. I silently screamed, releasing air pockets instead of noise, hoping that someone would hear me. I felt the current of the tide moving above me, a sign that Kalima had won: she would wash me away from existence so what was once my reality would become her own. The both of us could no longer coexist in this world, considering the histories from the past were now coinciding with the present.

"Help me..." I mouthed the words, but the sound found itself trapped in another cluster of bubbles. Why did I think that I was strong enough to takeback control over my body again? Once I allowed Kalima dominance, I did not realize that there would be no point of return. My thoughts quickly shifted to Cairo, and I wondered if my love for him had anything to do with Kalima. Was I only feeling what Kalima felt? Even after a millennium and a betrayal apart, her love for him never died. And could it also be the same for him?

All of this began with Cairo, and as I continued to sink to the dark depths of my own soul, I became aware that this could all end with him. Another memory washes over me.

Cairo and I had gotten into an argument earlier in the day, triggered by an insecurity of mine that I'd been fighting against since the day he and I first met. Throughout the few romantic relationships I experienced, the familiar, ice cold presence of anxiety filters into my psyche, magnifying my fears of rejection and the nightmarish but incessant mental comparisons to their exes. And when I found myself wrapped up in Cairo's arms, it would be no different; if anything, with him, it was worse. His rich honey brown skin, whiskey colored eyes, full lips, his fit muscular form, and not to mention the fact that his natural masculine scent reminded me of pinewood and hot sex.

On this particular evening, I stormed out of his townhome, jumped into my car and sped angrily down the 405 until I pulled into the safety and comfort of my own garage. His words had cut like sharp glass, right down to the marrow of my soul.

"Well, you can go Dinayra," he told me. The cold callousness of his direct nonchalant response towards my increasing annoyance with him. The details that led up to our argument that day are fuzzy. "Just go...," he continued, while my thoughts scrambled for a response. "I have more

important things to concern myself with than standing here arguing with you."

Well damn... I remember thinking to myself. Just as I stood there in the center of his bedroom, I was equally at a loss for words as I was emotion. From my experiences with men, this signified the ending of our entanglement; and it was foolish of me to even believe that there would be anything more than what was already experienced: his touch, his laughter; the bottomless depths of our conversations; the late nights and early mornings. Just like the seasons, our relationship changed, and it was best for me to leave with what dignity I had left.

"Fine," I said, quickly turning towards the stairs. "You will not have to worry about me...consider me gone."

He started to say something, but my feet had already propelled me down the stairs, out the door and into my car. Grief, humiliation, undesired vulnerability, and a plethora of other emotions pained me. I wished he had chased after me, trailed behind the very soles of my feet to stop me. But he didn't. I wanted him to yell and scream and then beg me not to get in the car. He didn't. Instead, he allowed me to drive away.

Hot tears poured down my face as I pulled out of his driveway. This is what he wanted, I fumed. The fine. It is what it is. Kalima had been silent throughout the earlier phases of me and Cairo's relationship and as I reflect deeper into this particular memory, now it all makes sense. Later on that night, after I spent three hours wallowing and crying on the couch, I ended up dragging my emotionally defeated carcass into the shower before climbing into bed. I was too exhausted to contemplate the fact that Cairo still had a key and too tired to have heard him come in.

I woke up to the tender caress of his fingertips along my spine and the warmth of his breath on my face. His body felt warm and welcoming and instinctively, I snuggled into his chest. He kissed me on my forehead, the bridge of my nose, my lips... Soon, I was wrapped in his arms, entangled in a wave of passion mixed in with unspoken forgiveness, insecurities that were contained and pushed back into the deepest pits of my mind...everything that remained unsaid echoed through each caress, tender kiss, until finally in the predawn hours we both collapsed. Our minds, our hearts, our bodies were completely spent. And even with sleep filled eyes, he found the strength to tuck me into his embrace and kiss me on top of the head before nodding off.

I remember that night like it was yesterday; and just like "yesterday", every ounce of love that I felt for Cairo reignited in me, jumpstarting my heart. It was like the strike of a match the lit the fibers of my soul ablaze. I went from sinking towards the endless fathoms of my soul, washed away, and drowned out by the tide of emotion to swimming towards the gateway of light that opened beneath me. As I swam closer, the pressure of the water felt more like a vacuum. There was no turning back now, even if I wanted to.

As I approached, now trapped within the boundaries of the whirlpool, I felt myself being flushed out of the realm that was once Kalima's. As I began the spin downward, my thoughts were still focused on Cairo.

"Cairo!" I managed to call out, my voice breaking through the barrier of water and echoing into the airwaves. I needed him to know that I was still fighting and that I was not completely lost. Maybe my voice would be a beacon for him to hold out hope and maybe, this was the hope that I needed. I opened my mouth to call out his name again, but the pressure from the void of light yanked me into the opening and the last thing I can remember is Cairo's face flashing before my eyes and the look of sudden awareness soon after I called his name.

Hope springs eternal: he heard me.

THIRTY-FOUR

Kalima

While Demelza busied herself with the task of opening the Veil, I followed the orbs of light that plummeted from the sky, in the northern most direction, towards what is known as modern day Yellowknife, a Canadian territory known for its main attraction, aurora borealis, also known as The Northern Lights. Moving through the atmosphere at a speed to quick for the human eye, the massive balls of light masked the hidden forms of entities as old as the concept of Time itself. I trailed behind them, even as they made their plummet into the earth's crust. Their collision created a miles wide cavern that ripped through the predominantly rocky landscape of the outskirts of town. The rumbling could be heard beyond the local mines and the rivers and lakes that contributed to the town's overall intrigue.

I landed just a few meters away from the smoke and haze. My footsteps echoed in the backdrop of the surrounding silence.

Sirens ignited in the distance in response to the gaping smoking holes in the ground. A helicopter hovered overhead and with my Scythe, I created a translucent shield to temporarily blind the curious humans from viewing the waking entities.

"I have come," I announced, taking position at the edge of the cavern closest to me.

A large hand shot up from the cavern, pushing the rest of the barely visible form of the entity whose mark on human history remained present to this day, however its origins a forgotten mystery. A dozen green serpents slithered up ahead of him, gliding their way towards me until they reached my feet and snaked a path around my ankles.

It took him several moments for him to completely rise to his six foot eight height, although not his full stature, he loomed over me like the monolith that he is.

"Kalima..." He whispered; neon green eyes examined me cautiously. "This form is quite becoming of you."

"She has been the perfect host," I shrugged. "It has been too long Ophiuchus," I said.

"It is not often when the Nine threatens all forms of existence," Ophiuchus. "Even the kingdom of Hell is preparing to rise for war."

The smoke slowly began to clear, revealing the midnight skin that was as dark as the sky, a chiseled brow, deep set green eyes and full lips. Broad shoulders over a lean frame, powerful arms which hung at his side. Gold plating covered his chest and lined the tips of his shoulders. On his hip hung a long blade and draped comfortably around his neck and torso was his companion, a green Boa. The gold staff that he held in his gripped sparked with electricity.

"So, this is the end times," came a soft murmuring from behind him. Orion, matching Ophiuchus in height and build, stood beside him. Through his irises I could see the galaxies from beyond,

210

kingdoms of stars stretching well into infinity. "It is different to witness the rise of humanity, but to stand in the midst of its accomplishments and failures...I have no words."

He took a moment to look around, his dark skin shimmering with dust from the stars, and his waist length locks shifting with the breeze. "So much has changed since the days I first walked the earth," he continued.

"Isis, I'm sure would say the same thing," I added.

"Ah my love...she would indeed. I told her, for her safety to remain where she is. I would be truly lost if I lost her to the Nine."

"We must be off," I said after a pause. "The battle has already begun..."

"I know...Titus is close to accomplishing his goal. Angelic blood has spilled..." Ophiuchus said, gripping his staff.

My fists clench as the images of Titus gripping a struggling warrior angel and ripping his wings from his frame while his concubine, Tethy's opened her jaws of darkness and consumed dozens of spirits in single swallow.

"They won't be able to hold the line much longer," I breathed. "We must go. Now!"

THIRTY-FIVE

Cairo

I examine the beautifully crafted blade, my thoughts drifting back to those final moments between myself and Kalima. She left a trail of destruction behind her which made it easy to find her. Foreign entities from neighboring realms sought to destroy her and the world that I had known them trembled with each step she took. Even the moon had turned red to signify the war of the realms. Several warrior angels had found themselves wounded from the wrath of her Scythe, which infuriated Michael even more. She decimated the few scattered Fallen Ones who managed to escape their punishments for violating Cosmic Law, their remains a warning perhaps to those who dared to challenge her.

During our short lived relationship, she never mentioned the pending threat of the Nine. There was no talk of entities that held dominion over realms that existed well beyond the heavens. She spoke of our lives together into eternity while simultaneously presenting herself as nothing more than a guest amongst my people. Had I'd known what she knew…of what was coming, I would have fought by her side instead of against her.

And now, as I continue to examine the Obsidian handle of the blade and recall the exact moment Archangel Michael dropped me from the air and just a few steps behind Kalima. Her rage was palpable; I could taste the bitterness of her soul, the saltiness of her tears as the wind carried them away. I knew she could sense my approach and even though I was sure she knew what I had come there to do, she kept her back turned to me. Bale strength winds threatened to send me off into a downward spiral off the cliff, but I maintained my resolve. What was done must be undone, as Michael had warned.

The sky had blackened with angry, dark clouds and lightening flashed across the sky. Mournful spirits called out to me as I inched closer to Kalima. Her Scythe had already left her grip and began its spin in a counter clock direction at an arm's length in front of her. For a brief second, our minds connected. I heard the wails of innocent women forced into submission under the wills of their abusive husbands; I heard the painful cries of the children, cry out in hunger, loneliness, fear…I saw the oceans crash and roll violently against the shore. I heard the earth cry out from the spilling of blood. I saw the wicked terrorize the innocent. But what I didn't see was that was all a vision of the pending doom resulting from the arrival of Titus and his twisted siblings.

Kalima's blood stained the earth because of me. Her power stripped from her and having gathered itself into the pages of a book which was nearly stolen by Azrael had it not been for Michael's interference. I could not help but contemplate how the Divine Plan, always orchestrated a path and found a way to ensure that regardless of what happened, she would return to fulfill her destiny. I tuck the blade back into the gold box, my mood darkening like the current settings of the sky.

"Cairo…" The faint whisper of Dinayra's voice calls out to me in the distance. I frantically search the room for the source of her voice. With the Veil slowly becoming undone by the presence of powerful entities like Kalima herself, from my experience, this could simply be the work of any trickster deity.

"Dinayra!" I yell, my voice bouncing off the four walls of my bedroom and ricocheting from my closet space. Nothing. There was no response. The only sounds to be heard were the rustling of the Sycamore tree against my window and the voice of the television reporter downstairs.

"D?" I say again, hoping that this time, she would hear me. *She's trying to come through,* I think to myself. *She has to be.*

I release a slow exhale to center my thoughts and to focus. As a Keeper, I have access to the other realms, and wherever Dinayra is, I am sure I can find her. The space between my eyes, where my invisible third eye rests, tingled and warmed as I connected with the Akashic Halls. The flooring was nothing more than a translucent path ignited by a lineup of stars. My feet echoed while I cautiously surveyed the labyrinth of corridors that seemed to stretch on forever. I had only been inside these Halls a few times in my existence, namely because I spent the last millennia determined to find Kalima's book to stop her awakening.

The last time I strolled through the halls, I was searching for clues to help me locate The Book of Obsidian. And now as I bypass another mysterious doorway, I realized I should have spent more time exploring the Akashic Halls. Part of a Keeper's job is to know how to navigate this sacred space of creation and knowledge. Harab understood this and had every intention of teaching me but unfortunately, fate had other plans.

I continued with my journey, moving further through the winding corridor, I noticed a dark shadowy like figure hovering over the walkway. It's dark robing flapped against its tall form. Its face was masked by the illusion of darkness. As I approached, I was left with the impression that it was waiting for me.

"It is about time, Keeper," it said. The entity's voice was neither masculine nor feminine, its tone rested somewhere in between. "Harab requested that I wait for your arrival, little did I know it would take a millennium for you to find me."

"Who are you?" I asked.

"I am the Guardian of the Halls," the entity declared. "My name is Rae." The Guardian paused and looked in the direction of the doorway closest to it. "What you seek is just beyond this door. Dinayra, correct?"

I nod my head but say nothing more. I watch as the Guardian hovers in closer to me; the closeness of its proximity brought an icy chill with it. Strangely, this particular entity could easily be confused with any one of the gods of death, but instinctively, I knew that it was something more than that.

"I am the line between Life and Death," it continued. "That is why you are here. Dinayra's spirit is lost between those spaces."

"I heard her voice calling out to me," I said. "I need to find her. How do I bring her back?"

"Kalima's war must be fought and won. If Kalima loses the battle with the Nine, Dinayra will -like life itself - be lost forever. She does have a greater purpose however, unbeknownst to Kalima, which is how and why I am able to help you."

"Well, we have to help her now!" I reached for the door only for the latch to be blocked by an icy hand.

"No," Rae said gently. "Only I can pass through this realm. Go fight. I will find Dinayra and for the time being, keep her soul here where it will remain safe. Help Kalima fight so that balance may be restored. Trust the Divine, Asir."

"I no longer go by that name," I said pointedly.

"I know that you prefer Cairo, however, that is not the name registered in my book of Keepers."

"How –

"Stop with the questions," Rae leaned forward with an index

finger and gently tapped me on the forehead. The softness of the contact held enough force to send me flying backwards. "Go. Finish what was started centuries ago and what was undone must now be complete."

Rae's voice echoed throughout every fiber and cell of my being and when my eyes snapped open, I was greeted by the colorless gaze of Michael himself.

"The battle has already begun," Michael stated grimly. His eyes veered over to the gold box that held the Blade of Babylon. "I take it you know what you must do."

"That I do," I sighed. "Let's finish this."

CHAPTER

THIRTY-SIX

Kalima

B lack lightning struck across the sky forcing migrating birds from the air. The earth rumbled, mountains shook, and the winds began to howl. The oceans cried out, they surged and thrashed about violently while her depths bubbled over with dark fury.

"Let them come to us," Ophiuchus mentally suggested. *"We could use the earth as a power source."*

"Follow me," I encouraged, taking the lead. We propelled ourselves through the ethers back to the tower where Demelza and Marjani awaited. Orion remained silent as he trailed behind me and Ophiuchus.

"Look behind you Kalima," Ophiuchus murmured, briefly turning his head. I quickly glanced behind me to find hundreds of thousands of bright blue orbs growing in number. They surrounded us, creating a blanket of light underneath us.

"Reapers," I murmured. "My precious Reapers have come to join us in this fight."

219

"As they should," Ophiuchus said evenly. "They always knew that you would return."

"It is a shame that I had to. I had found something that I once searched the galaxies for and could never find," I confessed.

"And what is that?" Ophiuchus asked.

"Peace."

"Ah...tis is a rare gift. Appreciate it for what it was. Peace will return to you..." He paused and shifted his gaze to the landscape beneath us. "Such a strange world. I've felt the wicked impressions, tasted the blood that spilled, and I've heard the wails from the earth herself crying out to the heavens for help."

"Yes," I agreed. "The echoes of her pain still reverberate through me. She is deeply wounded by the humans that inhabit her womb."

"May I ask you a question?" Ophiuchus asked, his gaze now fixed on the miles of sky ahead of us.

"Of course..."

"Do you believe that they are worth it?"

His question gave me pause, not because of the question itself, but because of my answer. "I have spent a millennium pondering that very question: is any of this worth it? They kill. They rape. Children are murdered by the hands of their parents. Women are abused by the very men sworn to protect them. Humans destroy *everything*...There is no balance. They have disrupted the nature of earth and have no respect for the system of things, let alone Cosmic Law..."

"So, I take that as a no," Ophiuchus chuckled.

"No, no, not entirely... the earth's pulse reflects the energies of all beings that are connected to her and not all humans are as corrupt and cruel as that infect this realm. Many of them are good and pure at heart - those are the ones I fight for and protect. It is only fair and just."

"And what about Asir?"

"Cairo," I add quickly. "I understand why he did what he did and now he understands why I do what I must do."

"Do you still love him even though he betrayed you?"

"He is still a good man, regardless of all that happened. Perhaps in another lifetime will we be able to surrender to the fullness of the love that was between the two of us." The familiar ache of sadness filled me, but instead of succumbing to the painful memories of a sordid past, I forced myself to remain in the present. Titus was perhaps minutes away from breaching the earth's atmosphere. What was done was done and must remain in the grave where it belongs. Besides, when all of this was over, Cairo would move on as he always has.

"I could never understand how you of all beings would fall victim to the rules of what humans call love," Ophiuchus said. "I would not have blamed you if you had razed the planet. But that is why I admire you Kalima and why also, I envy you. You were allowed to experience some of what humans' experience which may be the foundation of your empathy towards them. I am only here to because you called and because the earth needs me."

"Once this is done, I will be free. The Archangels can continue to watch over them and hopefully, while I am gone, they will not find another way to destroy themselves."

"Well don't hold your breath," Ophiuchus snorted. "They are designed to become their ultimate destruction – a stipulation of Cosmic Law to ensure balance."

We drift off into a companionable silence moments before I quickly advance ahead of them and materialize just outside of the fortress where Demelza and Marjani awaited. My legion of Reapers surrounds the fortress and disappears into the ethers, awaiting my command.

"Hmm, this is where it begins," Orion murmured when he materialized onto the brown grass that lined the overall terrain.

The charred remains of the dead witches still clung to the air, their magic having yet to disburse, left behind a negative charge.

"Indeed. It's the perfect place for a battle to avoid a significant amount of innocent human casualties," Ophiuchus added.

I left the two of them to their thoughts and looked up at the tower. I caught a glimpse of Demelza's form, her long locks billowing in the breeze, with her arms raised above her head, a pulse of white light emanating from her palms. The outline of the invisible barrier that separated the physical realm from the spiritual world. Warrior spirits, high priests and guides filtered through by the dozens, taking position around the tower. I could sense Marjani hidden inside the walls, her soft chants of protection creating runes that ingrained themselves on the outer walls of the fortress.

The sudden shift in the atmosphere gave me pause and spun around to look in the direction of the horizon where Orion and Ophiuchus held their gaze. An ear shattering whine shot through the airwaves, the force of the sound tore a path through the city of Axum; however, I dug my feet deeper into the ground to connect with the earth's pulse. The cries of humanity bubbled up through her and into me and I could see buildings in major cities collapse; the streets and sidewalks of the residential neighborhoods splintered.

Chaos erupted with screams and sirens. Humans poured out of the emergency exit points of the neighboring buildings. The vision shifted in the direction of the cosmos where I witnessed at least a hundred million stars collapsed on themselves, some of them increasing in mass in preparation for their own self destruction. The gamma rays from the sun intensified, reaching out like a whip in the direction of the approaching Nine, as if attempting to prevent them from successfully breaching the earth's atmosphere.

"Brace yourselves..." I murmured through grit teeth. "He's close..."

222

"I've been waiting to strip the tongue from Titus' jaws for centuries," Orion growled.

"Then let us work together to make sure that his voice is never again echoed in the cosmos," Ophiuchus said, the serpent that draped around his neck, slithered onto the ground before disappearing into the earth.

And then it happened: The Nine began to plummet through the atmosphere, piercing the sky like massive asteroids. I could sense the earth preparing for their impact. However, instead of colliding with the main city, they altered their course, moving at Mach Speed in our direction.

"And so, it ends..." I whispered into the breeze. The energy from my Scythe warms the palm of my hand. I inhale deeply and with the power from which I was created, I dematerialize into the ether, appearing directly in front of Titus in midflight.

"Kalima..." he growled, his abysmal eyes narrowing and igniting with a bright yellow.

"Titus. I have felt the dark tendrils of your wickedness from the depths of Saturn's womb. Your power has corrupted you and your followers. Eons spent on a lonely throne will drive any king mad."

"I am here for what is mine, Kalima. Give it to me and I shall find mercy for these wretched humans that you love so much."

"What is mine shall never be taken," I stated evenly. "But you are more than welcomed to try."

I maneuver myself above him and watch him strike the ground with the force of a meteor, creating a miles deep cavern. The rest of the Nine followed suit and as the world trembled at the arrival of the oldest entities in existence, I gripped my Scythe and concentrated the dark energy that fueled my soul.

"My Reapers," I called out. "Protectors and Guardians of the Dead and Karmic Debt. Our enemies have arrived. ATTACK!!"

CHAPTER

THIRTY-SEVEN

Azrael

Azrael was the last to touch down from the ethers and onto the rooftop of the tower where Kalima's witch, Demelza snatched a lightning bolt from the sky and hurled it at the incoming Calypso. Calypso, her eyes blazed with red hot fury screeched from the third-degree burns that covered her body and sent her spiraling downwards towards the battle that was taking place on the ground. Zavion, the mountain sized behemoth of a god struck Ophiuchus with a spiked whip which wrapped around the serpent deity's throat and forced him to the ground. The deity went down hard, his knees creating a deep cavern in the ground while rocking the earth, causing her to rumble outward for miles. The human populations were in a panic, scattering like vermin in all directions.

"Cover the humans!"

Azrael scoffed at the all too familiar sight of Michael and his valiant glory followed by a battalion of Archangels that dove downward from the sky to protect and shield the vulnerable

225

humans that were scurrying deeper into the city for cover. He frowned as he watched Michael fly head on in the direction of Atlanta and her massive hammer which she attempted to bring down on Kalima with. Kalima side stepped the swipe and channeled the energy from her Scythe and sent out a beam of concentrated destruction into Atlanta. The goddess had no time to contemplate her own demise as she exploded into pure ash which rained down over the landscape.

Orion quickly raised an invisible shield over the area to block out further human interaction and to prevent any human casualties while the war of the gods took place in the backdrop of Axum. Azrael maintained his focus on Kalima as he began to circle overhead. His own followers had already joined the battle, surrounding Orion, lunging at the old deity in droves. Azrael turned his head quickly enough to match the hard blow of the blessed blade from Michael's hand.

"I should have ended you a long time ago," Michael seethed through clenched teeth. He landed a smooth kick to Azrael's face, knocking his head backwards. Azrael quickly recovered and in a deft move, he swung his own dark blade which barely grazed the Archangel's jugular. Michael reared backward, stretching out his wings and flipped himself over Azrael's head and flew off in the direction of Titus.

"Son of a bitch," Azrael fumes, flying after Michael. "I will have your head before sunrise. That is a promise."

Michael's wings pressed against his muscled form as he torpedoed himself across the sky. He raised his blade high above his head and bellowed, "Kalima! Now!"

The moment seemed to occur in slow motion as Azrael stopped midway, ten thousand feet above the three of them, with chaos a symphony in the background. Black blood and ash rained from the sky and thick angry clouds had begun to close in. Michael lowered his blade at the same time black shadows burst

226

out from Kalima's shoulder blades to stretch out in the form of massive wings. Titus, the largest of the Nine, towered over the area, reaching a height of almost four stories but still moved with the speed of a bullet. However, his speed could not match their determination and Azrael looked on in horror as the sickled shaped end of her Scythe sliced through Titus's neck. Michael's blade connected with the giant's neck from behind and the deity's scream was soon silenced. His head plummeted from his shoulders and slammed into the empty row of abandoned houses.

"It's not over!" Kalima called out, doubling back. "His body can regenerate. This just gives us enough time to deal with the others as I wait for Saturn to complete its alignment."

That's right, Azrael thought to himself. *I still have time.* He nosedived towards the ground where he witnessed Ophiuchus engaging with Zavion in hand to hand combat. Azrael landed into a sprint, hoping to aid Zavion in taking out at least the serpent deity but was quickly thwarted when his gargantuan serpent burst from the ground rising to a colossal height. It's neon green scales glimmered even under the dimming light of the overcast sky. It released a high-pitched screech that overwhelmed a group of swarming Fallen and forced them to circle back and collide into each other. The remaining members of the Nine, dropped to their knees, desperate to cover their ears in hopes of silencing the snake's mind-numbing scream that echoed into the depths of the heavens.

The massive fangs that protruded from its mouth dripped a thick yellow acid that melted away whatever had the misfortune of encountering it. Its icy white stare surveyed the land before landing on Azrael. The Fallen entity glanced up at the looming shadow that the created casted overhead and in an instant, the snake hissed and charged in his direction. Azrael's wings spread out for him to take flight, but the massive jaws of the serpent clamped down on him, its fangs piercing through his chest and snapping his vertebrae. But instead of swallowing him, the serpent spat him out onto the dry grass and slithered off to pursue the other Fallen entities who were headed to assist in his direction.

With a groan, Azrael forced himself to roll onto his back where for a few seconds, he could gaze into the sky to make note of the celestial alignment that was threatening to turn the tide.

"I will defeat you Kalima," He growled as his wounds began to stitch themselves together. "I will *take* what is mine."

CHAPTER
THIRTY-EIGHT

Dinayra

I do not remember how or when I regained consciousness, let alone how I found myself wrapped in a warm blanket on a stack of thick bedding in front of a flickering fire. Fatigue still held me in its grip; opening my eyes was a struggle because my eyeballs felt like my lids were rubbing against sandpaper. I yearned to sleep for another thousand years; and the comfort from the blanket and the fire did not exactly help with the process of waking up either.

"I am glad to know that I pulled you out in time," came the soft voice of a hooded figure, who appeared out of nowhere in front of me. "There was a strong possibility that you would have been lost and that cannot happen."

"Who are you?" I grumbled, pushing myself up only for exhaustion to remind me that it was best that I lie back down.

"My name is Rae, and I am the Guardian of these here Akashic Halls. Between you and Cairo, the last twenty four hours have brought quite the excitement."

231

"Cairo is here? Where is he? I need to talk to him-

"Relax, he isn't here. He came here looking for you and I sent him on his way."

"But-

"Shh, you will need to conserve your energy. You have expended quite a bit swimming in the sea of your own emotion and fighting against the barriers of your own psyche. Here you will be kept safe."

"But I need to get back home!"

"I'm afraid I can't allow that to happen just yet," Rae told me, her voice remaining even and cool. "You were chosen long before your bloodline even began to be the host body for Kalima. Actions from the past had to be set right for humanity to survive and those in the upper realms could not risk you reclaiming your body at the worst possible moment. So, I put you here where at least, you have some reprieve. You are not sharing your thoughts or deepest imaginings with another soul. I would take advantage of the opportunity. Consider it a gift."

"I don't understand why any of this is happening to me," I groaned, turning on my side. Somehow, I got the sneaking impression that I was neither alive nor dead since I technically wasn't inhabiting my body.

"You are not dead. You are in a place where very few humans have ever had the chance to visit. Even the most powerful of Oracles could only wish on a distant star to be granted access to the Akashic Halls."

"The Akashic Halls?"

"Yes. This is the gateway to every world both imagined and created. History recorded from the mind of the Creator is kept here. Everything and everyone living, dead and existing in realms forbidden and forgotten is recorded here. Your past, present and future can be found here."

The more Rae continues to speak to me, the more exhausted I

become. I could barely keep my eyes open as she continued to define the Akashic Halls and its purpose, seemingly answering every other question except for why I am here.

"Sleep, child. You're here because your Fate was stolen from you by those who wish to destroy the balance of Life and Death; and your soul was deemed worthy for what is to come. When all is done Dinayra, I will bestow the gift that awaits you."

There was no resistance as sleep once again claimed me. There were still too many questions without answers; and it became increasingly apparent that time had run out. And as badly as I wanted to fight to hold on to my consciousness, I had no other choice but to finally admit defeat.

CHAPTER
THIRTY-NINE

Kalima

I could sense the convergence of energies involving the planets forming their alignment. Collectively, their power fueled me, which in turn, fed my army of Reapers. Carnage and bloodshed surrounded me as I charged at Tethys, who's magic darkened the sky with thousands of nine inch locusts. The sight of the invasion reminded me of the days of ancient Egypt, when King Ramses II had to endure the seven plagues as penance for not granting the freedom the Hebrew people. I remember watching it all take place from the small pools of water in my realm. I had hoped at that time to be released from my prison, even but temporarily just so that I could bring order to the chaos surrounding the Egyptian people. But I was forced to only bear witness of the story that begun to unfold.

"Reapers!" I called out, ducking out of Tethy's striking range. She reared back with, her silver strands of hair extending from her scalp like tiny whips, shooting out in my direction. A few of my Reapers found themselves trapped in her snares. She shredded their black wings, causing them to writhe in pain. However, her hold on them was temporary as one of them, released a hard flung of his sickle in her direction. The weapon sliced through her attacking tendrils and despite her attempts to thwart it, the sickle pierced her in the center of her face, plunging deeply into her skull. The entity screamed violently, her whiplike tendrils thrashing about, releasing some of my captured Reapers. I lunged in her direction, raising my Scythe high above my head and quickly landed the devasting blow to her neck, severing her head from her shoulders.

There was no time to enjoy watching her head plummet to the ground, to relish the image of her open mouthed horror looking downward before bouncing off the concrete and disintegrating into ash. The rest of her form collapsed from the sky, assuming the same fate as her head. I swooped down to aid Ophiuchus who was locked in a wrestling match with Zavion. The hulking deity with nebulae for eyes and a mouth filled with razor sharp teeth bit down on Ophiuchus's jugular. Ophiuchus' Serpent charged from underneath the ground, uprooting everything that had the misfortune of lining its path. I trailed above it, my energy darkening with my rage and the instant the serpent burst out from underneath the surface of the earth and surprised Zavion by delivering a spine snapping bite from behind, I plunged my Scythe into Zavion's neck. Black blood spurted out and the old god released his hold on Ophiuchus. The serpent continued to devour him while Ophiuchus pushed himself off the ground with a grunt.

"Whatever you do," I said with a half grin. "Don't die."

"Bug off," Ophiuchus grumbled. "I was just getting started."

"Well now that you've had your warmup, prepare for the alignment. I can already feel its energies filtering through me."

"So can I," Ophiuchus said, peering up at the sky. "The eclipse is upon us Kalima. We must do what we must before we find ourselves distracted in battle."

I turned my head off in the distance to find Orion's dark gaze melting a path through a line of Fallen angels that were charging in his direction. Castiel, one of the lower rankings of the Nine, attempted to land a surprise swing with his blade over Orion's head. In a quick and calculated move, Orion dodged the swing, returning one of his own with his dagger and plunged it deep within Castiel's chest cavity. Castiel cried out, capturing the immediate attention of the remaining Nine.

Demelza's chant echoed across the battlefield, her voice opened a gateway for spirit guides and low ranking deities to pass through, charged with their righteous outrage into battle. Marjani stood near the edge of the tower; her hands spread out pulsing with energy to maintain the invisible shield of protection over them. However, Marjani would not be able to maintain the barrier for much longer. And if any of the remaining Nine or Fallen attacked the tower directly, they would collapse in the rubble.

Reapers! I mentally shouted. *Protect the Tower! Let no harm befall Marjani or Demelza!*

I returned my focus onto Orion who had taken position near the entrance of the city with Ophiuchus. It was time. Gripping my Scythe tightly, I fold away into the airwaves and appear just in time to form a pyramid with Orion and Ophiuchus. The two of them remain on ground level, spread out by just six feet while I hover directly above them, my Scythe raised high above my head. Black lightning struck across the sky as the moon positioned itself directly in front of the sun. Orion's eyes blackened and within the depths of his irises, unexplored galaxies revealed themselves. His dark skin illuminated with a soft red glow and as he extended his opened palms, orbs of tiny clusters of stars filled them.

Ophiuchus slammed his staff into the ground, causing the earth to rumble and split. Neon green light burst through the large emerald that sat proudly at the tip of the staff. My Scythe jerked violently in my hand as his power connected with the energy that poured into me from the planetary alignment. Orion's power merged with Ophiuchus and together, we began to ascend towards the direction of the sky. Finally, it was happening. What was undone was to be finished. The Nine would no longer act as a threat not only against humanity but for all worlds to follow. The promise of a new beginning was being fulfilled -that is my purpose. I was created to rewrite the fabric of time and history and now as began to slowly spin my Scythe counterclockwise; the story of life and all of its beginnings and endings filled my vision. I witnessed the creation of stars and worlds; I watched as the hand of the Almighty spun a web that interconnected Life and Death across the Veil.

"Thy will be done," I whispered as my spinning staff increased in speed. The explosion that occurred throughout my body from the full power of Saturn's womb. Dark energies radiating from that of both Life and Death...the power of creation from the hand of the Creator pushed through my veins. I heard the screams and shouts from the angels; I felt the chime of steel meeting steel and then...

The world around me went black.

FORTY

Cairo

I arrived with the Archangels just as the battle had taken full swing. Michael and I landed in between two small buildings near the entrance of the city. A few frightened humans hunkered in a corner in an alley as the ground trembled again. Ash and debris rained from the darkening sky, while smoke permeated the atmosphere from the small, scattered mudbrick homes. The crumbled remains of rubble were a nightmarish reminder of the destruction that befell the city and a terrifying foreshadowing of what would happen to the rest of the world if Titus secured Kalima's Scythe. Michael immediately took flight to join his brothers in aerial combat. My sword remained sheathed at my side, while I held the Blade of Babylon tightly in my grip.

Another blast rocked the city and the loud cry echoed from the field. The roar shattered glass windows of the few standing buildings and abandoned cars that lined the vacant streets. The Blade of Babylon pulsed in my grip as I surveyed what was ahead of me and to my surprise, the decapitated head of Titus himself rolled into view, its size more alarming than its presence. The leader of the Nine's head was the size of a school bus.

Without a second thought, I sprinted through the side street until I reached the open field to find Kalima slicing through the tentacles of Tethys, guardian and goddess of the lost worlds. I stopped for the brevity of a second and watched Kalima instantly become lethal poetry. She was the movement of darkness on a starless night; she was death in motion acting in her element. Karma personified, goddess of darkness and destruction, her Scythe an extension of the justice she was created to enact, her sickle made a clean slice through the old goddess's neck, toppling her head from her shoulders. As her head spiraled to the ground, her black eyes shifted to a normal pale blue. Her screams pierced the airwaves before being silenced by the earth's crust.

Dark spirits appeared in front of me, their shadowy forms gathering in a spiral and lunging in my direction. I stabbed at each of their transparent forms, their shrieks stretched out for miles until they disappeared back to whatever dark void they emerged from. The nauseating scent of sulfur intensified as I sprinted in the direction of two massively built Fallen. Together they were locked in an attack from three equally built Reaper angels whose blue tainted skin glistened with sweat and blood from their enemies. My rage, fueled by memories of the massacre of my people, the elders, the children, the women – innocent lives that were stolen– aided me in the accuracy of my lunge towards the direction of the closest Fallen. His back was faced towards me as he focused on tearing the wings off of the Reaper he held pinned to the ground. With the Blade of Babylon, I pierced the entity's spine, using all of my strength the force the blade into his heart. With a hard shove from his powerful wings, I was air born. Had it not been for the quickness of one of the nearby Reapers who dove from the sky to catch me, immortal or not, I might not have survived the plummet to the ground.

The Fallen tore away at his back desperate to pull out the dagger, but within seconds he combusted into feathers and ash. The wounded Reaper managed to scramble away, his wings immediately growing back into place while the other collected the dagger and tossed it back to me. Chaos surrounded me as entities from every dimension joined the battle, including followers of the Dark Lord himself. Cosmic Law would not permit him and all his unholy power to join the fight as even under the law, it could not be determined which side he would fight for or against. Titus and the rest of the Nine would be too much of a temptation for another power grab; and when it was time for Humanity's final judgement, then and only then would his presence be allowed to exact his hand in this game of chess. Besides, Kalima's role was to only stop the Nine – at least for now.

And speaking of entity's, from the corner of my eye, I noticed one, albeit injured, trailing behind Kalima as she and the other two deities took position in the field. For the first time I was able to witness her in her true Reaper form: enormous black shadow wings had sprung out from her shoulder blades; concentrated violet energy surrounded her as she looked up towards the sky with her Scythe raised above her head. Off in the distance, I sensed Titus regenerating and if she could not successfully channel Saturn's power into her Scythe, all would be lost.

Now was my time to make things right. Even in the surrounding darkness, I could see Azrael creeping behind Orion, his blade ready to strike. *Let my dagger be swift and true*, I think to myself as I released the dagger from my grip and watched as it pierced through the airways like a bullet. Azrael lowered his blade to strike Orion from behind, however, my dagger sliced through the blade like butter and penetrated Azrael in the center of his chest. Lightning struck Kalima's Scythe, connecting Kalima, Ophiuchus and Orion in a triangle of power.

Azrael's curses filtered into the awareness of his Fallen

followers who left their respective opponents in the sky to dive to his aid. But it was too late, the Blade of Babylon caused him to implode from within. The explosion took out a few of the Fallen whom had swarmed in too closely, raining more black feathers and ash. I stood in the center of the blackened chaos, inhaling the smoke and ash that surrounded me. Harab, my former mentor appeared before me, his expression serene. He still wore the robbing of the original Keepers, the white linen wrapped tightly around him. What was once smooth dark brown skin was now a soft glow of light. He had ascended into the higher realms. He smiled warmly and for an instant, a flash of pride gazed back at me.

"Well done, Asir," He said to me.

"It's not over," I said grimly.

"I know. But I needed to tell you that you have made your people proud," Harab added. "Now, finish this. Finish what was left undone centuries ago. The spirits are with you. We can take care of the rest."

Harab vanished, his words still clinging to the air, wrapping around my thoughts and shifting my focus to Kalima's spinning Scythe. The ground continued to rumble as the war between ancient gods and spirits waged on. The speed of the Scythe accelerated, moving at Mach speed until it unleashed an ear shattering whining sound followed by a blast.

"Get down!" Michael ordered as he closed in on me from behind. He knocked me to the ground and covered me with his wings as a blast of light ignited, engulfing everything and everyone.

And then, the world, the universe and everything that I once knew, fell to black.

FORTY-ONE

Dinayra

"It is time Dinayra," came the familiar voice of Rae. "It is time for you to be reborn."

"What?" I asked groggily, struggling to fight through the grogginess of a peaceful sleep. "Did I die?"

"No, you are not dead," Rae chuckled softly. "Trust me if you were, you would know it."

She gently pulled the warmth of the blankets from around me and positioned me to sit forward.

"Come now. Kalima's purpose is now fulfilled."

"I can now go home?" I heard myself ask. I yawned deeply and every muscle in my body felt like jelly. I just wanted to crawl back into that safe space of bedding and sleep for another thousand years.

"Not yet. There is something I must do. Now get up."

Reluctantly, I pushed myself from the bedding and placed my feet onto the cold marble floor. Rae offered me her hands. "Stand up," she said. "Time is of the essence and if I am to do what has been decided to be done, we must not dottle."

On shaky knees I followed Rae out of the room and allowed her to guide me through the silent hallways of the Akashic Halls. The echoes of my bare feet slapping against the floor were the center of my thoughts. So much has happened in the last few days, this was all too much to process at once. And as my hooded tour guide continued to lead me into another passageway, her form hovering only a few inches from the ground, it made me wonder how I was able to even feel the warmth of her hands when she pulled me up.

"I can control my corporeal form," Rae said evenly. "I expend less energy when I am in an ethereal state."

"What would have been the alternative to me going home?" I asked, finally driven by curiosity. We paused at the threshold of another doorway before she turned around to reveal a pair of emerald, green eyes and skin as smooth and black as night.

"You would've just had to be reincarnated into whatever beginning was being created," she shrugged.

"And what's going to happen to Kalima?"

Rae held my gaze, and a sudden tranquility overcame me. "Kalima will return to Saturn's womb – no man or spirit or god will be able to harm her there. That is where she will remain until she is called again as is written in the Divine Plan."

"Can I at least talk to her?" I blurted out.

This time it was Rae who looked at me with surprise. "Why would you want to do that?"

I recoiled at her question, unsure of my own reasoning. "She's always been a part of me, and it will be strange to live on without her presence."

Rae continued to stare at me curiously before answering. "You know you are definitely one of the most interesting souls I've ever met. You will do well as a Keeper."

"A Keeper? Like Cairo?"

"Come along," Rae urged, turning around, and heading up another level of stairs. "You've acted as host to one of the most powerful entities in the history of creation and you thought that your journey in all this madness was over? You are special, Dinayra – always have been. I've watched you since your conception and you were no different than most humans being that you were granted a harder card in life than others. But the Divine had a plan for you…so prepare yourself for your rebirth."

Rae and I traveled up the flight of stairs, which I soon realized were not stairs, but a series of stars stacked upon one another. With each step we took we moved further away from the Hall of Records and deeper into a dark void, filled with thousands of stars. It was as if we were standing in the middle of a galaxy.

"We are," Rae said proudly. "Orion's belt to be exact. He would be happy to know that you had come."

Rae walked ahead of me until she stood atop a giant red dwarf and beckoned for me to approach. I cautiously took my time with my approach, uncertain if my next step would lead to an endless fall to my doom.

"You won't fall," Rae encouraged.

Still, I nervously took one step at a time until finally, we were but an arm's length apart.

"Rest your hands in mine," she said presenting her palms to me. "Mine will remain face up, yours face down."

I did as she instructed, once again surprised by the heat which radiated from her.

"I'm not a ghost you know," she chuckled. The heat from her palms increased until both of our hands ignited with a soft blue light.

"Allow the energy to flow into you and through you Dinayra… embrace its cleansing power, allow it to wash through you and over you…"

The calmness of Rae's voice pulled me into a trance. I did as she instructed: I allowed the power of the blue light flow into me like a gentle stream. Every hurtful memory was not erased, but the pain of it stripped away. The energy went deeper into my psyche, spreading out and coursed through my blood. Visions from memories of those who came before me filtered into my mind; ancient secrets, dark truths, histories that were long forgotten and buried under the foundation of lies became one with me. I witness Kalima's birth from the depths of Saturn's womb soon after the original Nine were locked away in their hidden realms. Protectress, karma, Reaper of Reapers, the spirit of the divine darkness of the feminine – that is what she was.

"When you awaken," Rae said, inching closer to take hold of me. "All that you once knew will exist no more. Sleep, Dinayra, so that your spirit may travel through the Keeper's Door."

I felt my body go limp in her arms and the moment my eyes closed, I saw myself falling once again. But rather than nearly drowning in an ocean of sorrow and bad memories, I plummeted through an infinite sea of stars, worlds that had yet to be discovered by man, and then for a split second, I saw Kalima with Scythe in hand and righteous fury burning in her eyes. She regarded me with a sad and knowing smile before turning away.

Finally, I understood and finally, she and I were both free.

CHAPTER

FORTY-TWO

Cairo

I have no idea how long I was out, but I woke up next to Dinayra, on top of her queen sized bed. She was sleeping soundly, peacefully, her mouth slightly opened allowing gentle snores to filter in and out. Am I dreaming? Carefully, I cradled her into me. The warmth of her skin confirmed that this was indeed real. But how? Where was Kalima? The Nine? What happened? She groaned but remained in her state of rest. The rise and fall of her chest eased some of my discomfort and I could not help but selfishly enjoy watching her sleep. I had never seen her so serene; most of her nights were spent waking up to cold sweats from her night terrors. And then I noticed something, in the center of her forehead, was a small branding – no bigger than that the size of a dime – but yet still noticeable. Kalima's symbol sat proudly on display – the mark of a Reaper. A cold rush of terror washed over me. Should I wake her? Did Kalima successfully merge with her and now has permanent dominion over –

"She's fine," Michael said, materializing in full form in front of her bed. "But she will be out for a while."

Gently, I pulled myself away from her to give myself room to sit up. I regarded the Archangel curiously, his colorless eyes lit with amusement.

"All is well," he said after a beat.

"Can you please tell me what happened?"

"The universe owes Kalima, Ophiuchus and Orion a major thank you and an apology it would seem – especially Kalima," he began, smoothing out the lapels of his navy blue suit. "She reset the balance of Time and obliterated Titus and the remaining Nine gods. Unfortunately, with the Nine no longer maintaining the order of their realms, there is a bit of chaos clean up that some of us like myself have to clean up."

"I see..."

"Afterward, Ophiuchus used his staff to reset the earth's energies and bring some healing to this cursed planet. It's like pushing a cancer back into remission if you ask me, and it's only a matter of time before it returns, but hey I don't make the rules. Orion closed out the portals before returning to his own seat in the heavens to restore some of the cosmic order. And Kalima, well... her Reapers offered her an honorary escort back to where she belongs. She collapsed soon after the fight and they collected her spirit and reunited her with her power source."

"So, it is done?" I ask, holding my breath.

"For now. As you of all people know, nothing is ever really finished. It's just that the Nine are no longer a concern. And one more thing," Michael added, his smile widening.

"Dinayra has been initiated as a Keeper. She has been assigned the responsibility of guarding a couple of very important books."

My jaw dropped. Holy hell, had this been the Divine Plan the entire time? "Wh- which books?"

"Well, Ophiuchus is in a bit of trouble now that he has revealed

THE BOOK OF OBSIDIAN

himself to the rest of the world. Gabriel and my other brothers did what they could to scrub away human memories of what recently happened. For the most part, humans are blaming a meteor strike and the collision of an asteroid for the damage that incurred in Axum and in other parts of the world. But there are those who are 'gifted' and unfortunately, we can't exactly do anything about that."

"So how is Ophiuchus in trouble?"

"Humans are not supposed to know the truth about who he is or that he even exists. It's too dangerous of a threat for an entity like him and with us being so close to the Armageddon, nothing is to be left to chance. And there are still those who exist who seek power and if you thought the likes of Titus getting a hold of Kalima's Scythe was guaranteed destruction, it's a far more terrifying thought to think of what someone would do if they were to successfully harness Ophiuchus energy."

I glanced back at the sleeping Dinayra, worry taking root in my mind and clouding my thoughts. "She doesn't deserve this..."

"She's a lot tougher than you are giving her credit for," Michael countered. "She survived. Think of it. She and Kalima – one of the most powerful entities in the history of the cosmos- fought for dominance and look at her. She is alive and well. She was found worthy to be chosen for the job – and get this..."

I massage my temples unsure if I wanted to hear any more. Dinayra had already been through enough. I had hoped that she would be allotted the rest of her human life to exist in peace. No more headaches, no more suffering. She could live the life of her choosing – that is what I had hoped for her- what I had fought for.

"She still shares a bit of a link to Kalima's power – something that will come in handy when whoever is after the book discovers who and what she is," Michael added.

"Oh God..."

"But hey, no sweat that's what she's got you and Demelza for...

and Marjani will be offering her assistance in training her in the ways of a Keeper."

My Dinayra, my sweet Dinayra... "Ok..."

"I mean, are you not up for the job? Because..."

"No, no, no... No one is going to protect her better than me."

"Now that's more like it," Michael perked. "Well look, I must go. Archangel business, you know?"

I frowned. "Of course."

"Call me if you need anything."

"Will do," I sighed.

Michael dematerialized into the air, leaving me alone with my thoughts. Dinayra was now the Keeper of Ophiuchus' book, which meant that he was no longer hidden in the darkest spaces of the sky, out of sight from human eyes and technology. He was here on earth, somewhere...living as a god without power. And Dinayra would guard the source of his power until it was time...

Son of a bitch. Michael was right, this shit *never* ends. But where was the book?

As soon as the thought crossed my mind, the heavy slam of the thick book with neatly pressed gold pages rattled her dresser.

"Fuck..."

EPILOGUE

Dinayra

"Be strong Dinayra." Kalima's voice whispered in the backdrop of my mind. *"I will always be with you. Call me when you need me."*

"But where are you going?" I asked, extending my hand out in the fogginess of my brain. I needed to connect with her at least one more time. There was no way this could be our goodbye.

"I have fulfilled my purpose and it is time for you to begin yours...."

"But-

"I must go. Be brave Dinayra..."

My eyes snapped open and inhale deeply. Everything felt familiar, the bed, the decorations that I bought from Ross and an online boutique a few years ago hung to the walls of my bedroom. I was home. I looked to the right of me to find the warm welcoming eyes of Cairo watching me. His smile calmed the mounting storm of confusion and anxiety threating to run freely on my nervous system. I sit up and he positions me to lay my head on his shoulder.

259

"I have so much to tell you…" I sighed.

"Me too…" He breathed.

"I don't know where to begin…"

"Me neither."

"Kalima is gone."

"I know."

"I was in the Akashic Halls, and I met Rae. She said you were there too," I said weakly.

"I was looking for you. I heard you call me. I thought I had lost you forever," he whispered. "I'm so sorry D, for everything."

I released another exhale and without thinking, I gently rubbed the center of my forehead where the brand sat. It was still tender to the touch, and I realized in that moment how my life had drastically and permanently changed. My entire life was centered around "becoming"; everything made sense. And it was a relief to fully understand that in this moment, my purpose had always been bigger than my pain.

"I'm a Keeper now," I said. "And before you say anything, I am fully aware of my responsibilities."

"Oh really."

"Yes. And you want to know what else that I know?" I asked sheepishly.

"And what is that?"

"That after being locked away in my own body and having to face myself, my fears and insecurities and just all of my mess, it was all part of a perfectly orchestrated Divine Plan."

"You sound like someone else I know." He kissed me on top of the head and another wave of peace flooded over me.

"And you know what else I know?" I turned my face up to look at him. I appreciated the depths of his eyes, his chiseled chin and honey brown skin.

"What is that?"

"I love you."

His eyes lit up and he leaned in and kissed me deeply. As a matter of fact, he kissed me like his life depended on it.

"I am never going to let you go," he vowed once we came up for air. "Ever."

"Good. I don't want you to."

Together, we pause and for no reason whatsoever we burst out in laughter, something that we both needed. Wiping tears from my eyes, I glanced over at the large tome that rested on my dresser, the weight of my new reality settling in.

"Is that the book?" I asked, point at it.

"Yup."

I inhaled deeply. "Fuck."

Cairo burst out another hard laugh before giving me another quick kiss. "My thoughts exactly."

ABOUT THE AUTHOR

Delizhia Jenkins is an Urban Fantasy and Paranormal Romance author who currently resides in Inglewood, CA. Her love for writing began in elementary school when the passion for storytelling developed into a journey of writing. Over the years, she honed her craft for storytelling and the written word by excelling in subjects such English and English Literature; and by indulging in her favorite past time which involved reading the works of Anne Rice, K'Wan, Christopher Pike, Carl Weber, and Omar Tyree. J.R. Ward's *Black Dagger Brotherhood* also claimed her heart, right along with fellow fantasy romance author Karen Marie Moning.

Miss Jenkins began publishing in 2013 with her first African American romance novel, *Love at Last.* After that, it was realized that her true magic rested in her writing about the ancient, the esoteric, and the supernatural. Moreover, since 2014, after her release of *Nubia Rising: The Awakening*, Miss Jenkins remained true to herself and her calling. And of course, being a true romantic at heart, it was important for her to fuse romance with the paranormal with a dash of "color." Miss Jenkins prides herself on writing for "the woman without the fairytale" and of course bringing magic and melanin to each book she writes.

Join my email list: missjenkinsbooks.com
Follow me on:

instagram.com/miss_jenkins_books

tiktok.com/@authordelizhi